Giles, Kenneth

Bardel's murder

BARDEL'S MURDER

BY THE SAME AUTHOR:

THE FUNERAL WAS IN SPAIN

HERE LIES MY WIFE

A HEARSE WITH HORSES

THE LEAD-LINED COFFIN

AN ENTRY OF DEATH

DEATH PAYS THE WAGES

NO BETTER FIEND

BARDEL'S MURDER

by

EDMUND McGIRR

WALKER AND COMPANY
New York

All the characters and events portrayed in this story are fictitious.

First published in the United States of America in 1974 by the Walker Publishing Company, Inc.

ISBN: 0-8027-5293-4

Library of Congress Catalog Card Number: 73-90392

Printed in the United States of America.

10 9 8 7 6 5 4 3 2 1

I

AS HAPPY AS a man who had to make provision for a wife and eight children can be, Timothy Bardel sang about honey-bees and snow-white turtle-doves as he tooled the non-descript little blue van westward. It was a fine June morning and Bardel, a sharp-looking man of forty-seven, expected to turn a profit of thirty-five pounds in untaxable pound notes. Not that Bardel was particularly dishonest: indeed part of his income came from his activities as a freelance enquiry agent. It worked in well with a little dealing in antiques which he regretfully had to pursue on a quick-turnover basis, a man of his marital status having little opportunity to accumulate capital.

In last week's trip to the north, negotiating between a respectable citizen and a clerk who had photostats of his employer's private file, he had stumbled on a small terrace of houses being demolished. Bardel had stopped his van, and with a dealer's expertise had become acquainted with the builder's foreman in charge of their destruction.

"Used to be attached to the old Castle—a manor house really. It's a school now. The servants lived here when they were pensioned off. The family died out in 1917 when the old Hun killed the four sons. It'll make a nice little block of flats and a supermarket."

There were bits and pieces of furniture scattered around, including a broken piano. The foreman grinned. "When things got old in the Castle, the cast-offs came down here. Broken-down furniture for broken-down scullions and 'Oh, thank you, me lady!' But they got their comeuppance thanks to Jerry and old Lloyd George."

Bardel had guffawed, but meantime his little grey eyes had been searching. "The wife and me bought a little shack by the sea, just two rooms. We won't use it more than two weeks out of the year until we retire, so I'm on the look-out for some cheap furniture, though God knows nothing seems cheap."

"The Common Market," said the foreman, "but nobody would listen to Harold's awful warnings, so now you can't afford a chair for your arse."

"There's six old 'uns over there," had said Bardel.

"Christ! Go back centuries," said the foreman, and Bardel inwardly winced. "Full of bloody borer, I'll be bound."

"I'll give you a pound and take 'em away."

"Make it double."

They compromised.

The chairs in fact had been made about 1760: not chairs for the gentry, but the stuff that went into the dark servants' hall. Four were in excellent order but the legs of two had been patched. Bardel reckoned he could get seven pounds each if he authenticated the purchase. Over the years his middleman had been a certain Julius McGregor who kept a large shop at Frippingham, in the Stockbrokers' Belt. Some effort had been made to town-plan, and the original part of the village was closed to traffic. It was in this that McGregor had acquired a four-storey house, dating from 1820, originally built by the local miller out of Napoleonic War profits. The ground floor and cellar comprised the shop. The first floor was McGregor's home, and the other two levels were transformed into four modern apartments.

One of the charms of the antique trade being the fact that shop assistants are not essential, McGregor relied on the services of one only, a retired school-teacher named Mr Snegg, who obliged when required. McGregor opened his shop at eight, when a scrub-woman did what was necessary in the cleaning line.

It was eight fifteen when Bardel, his van parked, opened the door, with its tinkling bell. "Hallo, there, Mac!"

No reply.

Funny, thought Bardel. He stood there for a few minutes until the shop door tinkled. It was the cleaner, a skinny woman.

"Is Mr McGregor in?"

"Why shouldn't he be?" He remembered that she was an uncommunicative, sharp-tongued shrew. The woman vanished through the back of the shop and presently he heard the sound of a bucket being filled. But then there was silence. Bardel wandered around, picking up a few objects and examining them. Nothing McGregor dealt in was trash, and that was why people paid his price, generally high. He thought he heard voices in the distance. "Hell," thought Bardel. He'd go and get a bit of breakfast, having only had coffee before departure from home.

He was going to the door, when a hard-faced man, the first of three, came through it, the bell jangling madly.

"Keep your hands in sight!"

Bardel obliged and they expertly frisked him.

"Blood on his cuff," said the youngest.

"I don't know what this is about, but I'm Timothy Bardel with a wallet full of papers to prove it."

"Keep him, Bean," said the hard-faced man. Bean looked as though he liked to use the muscles which made his serge coat bulge, so Bardel, though himself knowing certain tricks, kept quiet, looking at a set of mid-Victorian water-colours. There was a new vogue for them, he reflected, and made a mental note of it.

A quarter of an hour passed. McGregor's office was behind the shop. Once the skinny cleaner peered out at Bardel. Then the hard-faced man came out. "I'm Deputy Inspector Feld. I want you to follow me."

In the office the late Julius McGregor, a small, balding man, was seated behind the desk, propped against it, with his throat cut. There was a great deal of blood.

"You don't seem shocked."

"I'm a private detective," said Bardel heavily. "We do not see the sights you fellows do, but we see some. I am actually shocked. I knew Julius for, oh, I guess eighteen years."

"You had an appointment with him?"

"I just dropped in. I do a little dealing and had six chairs to sell him. They are in my van a couple of blocks away."

"A private eye and a dealer," said Feld with a humourless bark of laughter.

"I've got eight children and know something of antiques. Moving about as I do, I sometimes spot a bargain. I often sold to Julius, though of course his speciality was old silver."

"What would his stock be worth?"

"He once told me that he had a floating insurance for forty thousand. He kept the silver in a vault in the basement: some pieces would be worth up to a thousand pounds. Julius only acquired the really big-priced stuff when commissioned."

"How did that blood come on your cuff?"

"The shop's dark. Julius watched pennies and only turned the lights on when somebody came in. I must have touched something. I remember looking at a fine set of French carving knives."

"Very convenient. Bean!"

"Sir?" said the muscular man.

"Take Mr Bardel up to deceased's apartment. I trust that as a private eye and a dealer you will not object to co-operating."

"Not at all." But Bardel felt uneasy.

There was a door and a stairway next to the shop; but from the office there was what had been the old servants' staircase. The transformation had been ingeniously done, with the apartments quite self-contained. Constable Bean pushed past Bardel with a key.

"Better go into his study," suggested Bardel. It was to the right off the hallway, with three nice armchairs and shelves of books, every one concerning antiques or art, because McGregor had read of nothing else.

"Been here before, have you?" asked the constable.

"Many times," said Bardel, studying him. Not unintelligent, he thought, in spite of the brawn and general attitude of a frustrated stud ram. If he ever had eight children, thought Bardel wryly, he'd be calmer even if more irritable. He probably modelled himself after the hard-nosed Feld. The Inspector often influences the attitude of the younger men. He got out his wallet. "You might inventory that. We could be some time."

Bean produced a notebook and got to work. When he had finished Bardel said: "I don't mind questions."

"You are carrying a hundred pounds," said Bean.

"I told you I do a little dealing and a deposit in cash is always welcome. And as for the enquiry-agent business, you never know how long you might be away from home, and there is sometimes the odd fiver to grease a sweaty palm—divorce work mostly."

"Pays well?" asked the constable.

"As a man with a large family, I have to work for others, so much a day. I average four days a week, keeping my price low. Then there's a little jam from the dealing."

"Hot stuff?"

"Not much of that goes through the dealers. Oh, I guess you get some small articles that have been swiped, but generally they want some authentification."

"Did McGregor?"

"He was honest. If he asked too much, well you were a mug to pay it and he profited by his knowledge. I'm sure he did not buy hot goods, partly because most of his connection was of the carriage variety, mostly people who knew their antiques."

"In other words, not many casual customers?" Bean was openly taking notes.

"I imagine so. In this business people come in looking for some article worth up to, say, thirty pounds, for a wedding or birthday present or because perhaps they've seen it in the window and liked it. I saw some nice jewel boxes downstairs, Viennese I thought, well worth the money as a romantic present to a young lady." He thought Bean was not the man to make romantic presents to young ladies: a washing machine for his intended perhaps.

"What were you seeing him about?"

"I have six eighteenth-century chairs to sell."

"Eighteenth-century." Bean was impressed. "They'd be worth a bit."

"They are servants' hall stuff. I was going to start at forty-five quid for the lot, but come down much lower. As a buyer Julius loved to haggle: it was the breath of life to him. He'd practically tear his hair out over sixpence."

"A Scot, was he?"

"He was born on the Prussian border, near Poland. His father was a dealer in jewels. They—the father, mother and Julius—got out in 1935, when Julius was twelve." Bardel sighed and remembered McGregor's account of surreptitious meetings with venal, insolent officials who in return for the stock-in-trade granted a passport, the terror in case of a double-cross, and finally the arrival in Basle, the first stage to London.

"The father got a job with a wholesale jeweller's supply house. His name was thick Polish, so he changed it. Julius served in the Army, interpreting, then bought a barrow. He was a good dealer and ended up here. He had no relatives as far as he knew, the parents having died, and was a man who lived for business."

"No women?"

Bardel shrugged. "We never talked about women. As the father of eight, the subject has not much appeal to me."

"And you were on good terms with him?"

"Julius was a friend. You see, as a very small dealer, I was no opposition. He granted me no favours, but he could talk freely. His business is rather a skin game."

They sat in silence until Bardel said: "Better search me, I freely give permission." He removed his coat and trousers.

The constable was competent and thorough. "Nothing on you," he said at length, grudgingly. "Except that stain on your cuff. Your one mistake, eh? Why not confess and get it over, pal, the relief is very great."

"I did not kill the bloody man!" shouted Bardel, suddenly feeling exhausted.

"So that's how you thought of him!" said Inspector Feld, coming through the opened doorway.

"A figure of speech," said Bardel as the redness of his face subsided.

"As you said," Feld continued, "we found splashes of blood on a carving knife in the shop."

"I merely suggested it."

"No objection to having your finger-prints taken?"

"None."

The Inspector produced a kit from the black bag he carried

and afterwards solicitously swabbed Bardel's stained finger-tips with spirit.

They sat down. Bardel could hear vague noises around the apartment.

"Mr Bardel has given me an interesting account of deceased, sir," said the constable. "There are various business cards, a car licence and one hundred pounds in his wallet."

"The notes were bloodstained, of course," said Feld, eyes fixed slightly over Bardel's head.

"I suppose that will be for the lab, sir."

Bardel started to say something, but stopped.

"Tell me, Bardel," said the Inspector, "do you know the four tenants?"

"Slightly. There is Miss Traylor, of private means, Captain Joyningstowe—he is the rare-book shop of that name near Oxford Circus—Mr Snegg, a retired teacher who helped out in the shop, and a Miss June Smith, an art teacher who wants to learn about antiques."

"So they know you?"

"Of course."

"Very good!" The Inspector went to the door. "Miss Traylor, please."

Miss Traylor's weakness was for cheap wine, which she often declared had been prescribed by her specialist to assist her blood. She was seventy, looked older, and received a fair pension from the family business—a finishing school for young ladies in Switzerland where she had taught for thirty years. This was largely hearsay to Bardel, but he knew that she was not at her best at this hour. Excitement seemed to have effected what it generally took two cups of British burgundy to accomplish, and in her flowing green dressing-gown she was pretty steady.

"That is the beast," she declaimed. "Many a time I've heard him threatening to cut poor, dear Julius's throat."

"He knew you used to creep down the back stairs and listen," said Bardel. "Look, Inspector, McGregor and I had a kind of game. I usually brought any stuff in of an evening. We used to shout and insult each other. I was a money-grabbing shark, he was a dirty old Shylock who should have been shot. Afterwards we'd settle up and have a drink—Julius used to pick up an occasional parcel of Marsala to which we are—were—both partial."

"Drink and threats!" said the Inspector dismally. "Well, thank you, Miss Traylor. I'm afraid we'll have to have you at the 'quest."

"It looks very bad, Mr Bardel," he said when she had gone. "I must warn you that I have a strong suspicion. Any communication you have made was voluntary, but I should not make any more. The enquiry will be on Wednesday, day after tomorrow. Coroner usually starts at ten. I'd have legal representation were I you."

The red-haired man known as Piron was in his small office at the Agency. It was one in the afternoon and he was cogitating lunch. At his small service branch of the giant New York Agency, things were looking up, though the Old Man had decided, on patriotic grounds, not to pay more to staff operating in foreign countries. Six divorces, seven travellers'-cheque offences, and nine investigations of references were on his work-load. And that morning, at nine o'clock, he had seen an official of the Bank of England, a wizened man at an inlaid desk, a Turner behind him, and a secretary with best Wedgwood for the tea.

"Forgery," Piron had said. "That's a police matter."

"It has been a police matter for fifteen years, before I occupied this office. A Mr Six by Six. Each day he cashes six forged pound notes, pausing only on Sunday, possibly from religious scruple." He coughed and clawed off a scab from his bald head in appreciation of the small jest. "I dare say, Mr Piron, that the amount involved is not great: but it niggles. And of course, whatever we do, the good news spreads. Two youths were caught only last week experimenting in the photo lab of a technical college.

"You see, counterfeiting a note is amazingly easy after a few weeks' study at a good public library. A man in Australia, with no technical knowledge, did the same thing for ten years and was only caught by a prying landlady. The numbers remain the same, of course, but who looks at the number of a one-pound note?"

"The paper?"

"Oh, yes, against a light you can spot it, but on the Continent, Belgium in particular, you can pick up fancy paper which will deceive any busy shop-keeper and maybe a bank teller."

"Six a day."

"Yes, Mr Piron. Supermarkets over South London, *as far as we can tell.* Occasionally a race-course or an agricultural show."

"No clues at all?"

The banker shrugged. "If any sharp-eyed, overworked cashier spotted it, the passer would mumble some excuse and change the note. Two were detained by a supervisor over the past year. One was a housewife who had won it at the local betting shop: the other was a street trader. Both houses were searched, but they had obviously acquired the counterfeits in the normal course of trade. But," he tapped the table, "look at this photostat."

Piron peered. In what appeared to be ballpoint was the lettered word 'McGregor'.

"Sometimes it seems that half the population are named McGregor," he said.

"Your Agency is our last card. We have not much to lose. Somebody at the Yard suggested the man might be an American —there was a case in Chicago during 1945."

They settled terms for three months' work and a fat bonus for arrest and conviction. Then he saw a Government Security printer who said: "We never like to broadcast how easy it is, Mr Piron. Of course, you could produce an unforgeable note, but it might cost more than its face value."

"What kind of equipment would he require?"

"Very little of it." The printer unlocked a steel cabinet. "This is a three-hundred-word memorandum I prepared. You must read it here, for I am forbidden to let it out of sight."

"It seems very easy," said the red-headed detective at length.

"We just might get him through the stuff he has to buy—I gather the Forgery Branch do what they can—but it is very remote. Large quantities of forged notes are easy to detect, because the person who tries to pass, say, ten thousand pounds over a short time stands out like a sore thumb. The small ones are a bother and a great irritant and danger. But getting back to what he needs, the first is a close tongue, the second is a room he can keep locked. Most of them become careless, and an informer turns them in. This one has gone on too long for our comfort."

"Sure it is only one man?"

"It might be a family, but the technique is identical: that I'll guarantee."

Piron's elderly secretary stuck her head through the door. "Mr Bardel's here."

"What does *he* want?"

"He said it was urgent."

"Show him in." Piron was puzzled for Bardel was not a bothering type.

The foxy-faced man came directly to the point. "I think I'm going to be arrested for murder."

"Sit down and report." Piron tilted back in his chair and listened. Finally he said, "Are you sure this Julius McGregor was not a crook?"

"I'd take my oath he wasn't."

"He seemed to have accumulated a tidy sum. I suppose he owned the freehold?"

"Either that or a very long lease, but he was shrewd and perpetually working. I gathered he had a few strokes of luck when he was in his early thirties."

Piron thought. The Agency motto was to give employees, even part-time ones, help in times of trouble, but he would have recoiled from a murder case except for the name of McGregor.

"I'll go down and take a look," he said. "Any leads?"

Bardel scratched his sharp nose. "Julius might have been on to something. Oh, I knew when he was hugging a secret. I wondered whether it was forgery."

Piron's face stiffened in spite of himself. "Forging what?"

"With the boom in antiques, the forger has come into his own. Mind you, a hundred-year-old forgery, and there are plenty, is valuable as such. God knows how much the Italians and French turned out, not to mention the Spanish. Of recent years there has been a fair bit of it, furniture included. Get a matured bit of wood and 'age' it by flogging it with a bicycle chain. That's the start, but it is mainly a trap for beginners or those with seventy quid to spend. A lot of wood comes in from Spain, demolished farmhouses or churches destroyed in the war there. However Julius specialised in silver, something I don't know much about apart from the markings. I have heard a little talk that there is too much old silver coming on the market, good stuff, but without much authentification. 'Property of my grandpa who picked it up in Verona' or 'Smuggled in by a Hungarian refugee'. The workmanship is usually continental, but no expert that I know of has said straight out it was not genuine. Silver is difficult to tell by scientific tests: you'd work with old silver coins, plenty of them hanging around the Middle East. It would be a highly skilled job."

"An old-silver factory!" said Piron. "You know I read somewhere of the unexplained murder of a young silversmith in Portugal. About six months ago. It was thought that the guy—a Swiss on vacation—had got into a fight, and . . ." Piron stopped briefly ". . . by God if his throat was not cut ear to ear."

"I don't think they've got quite enough against me," said Bardel, "there was only this tiny smear of blood on my sleeve."

"There have been cases when a skilled killer avoided more than a few spots. All right, Tim, I'll go down now. Were you followed here?"

"Nobody follows me if I don't want it."

"I wouldn't pry around except by telephone from your home.

If we have a professional cut-throat around we'd better leave him to the police."

Piron drank a pint of milk and ate two dry biscuits and drove to Frippingham. There were signs of intense activity—you didn't get murder every day—but he finally got in to see Inspector Feld. Piron produced a document, presented to him by a grateful Home Office two years before. "I'm representing Mr Bardel."

"As what?"

"You know that I am a private enquiry agent."

"We prefer a solicitor."

"In fact I am a member of the New York Bar."

"I'm afraid an American lawyer . . ." The Inspector spread his hands.

"You had better not argue law with me, sir, otherwise I shall have to sweat up to the Home Office. Bardel is entitled at this stage to have a friend representing his interests."

Feld looked taken aback. A youngish man on the way up, thought Piron.

"What do you want? It seems very black against Bardel."

"Have you the photographs and preliminary medical reports?"

Silently Feld pushed a file over. Piron studied it for a few minutes. He said, "The throat was slashed from right to left."

"That is the path report."

"And therefore done by a right-handed man."

"I don't see . . ."

"This kind of killing is invariably a back-handed swing with the weapon. McGregor was seated facing the killer. Work it out!"

"That's for the experts."

"You might tell them that Bardel is completely left-handed. He would have slashed from left to right."

"A bit tenuous, eh?"

"I do not think so, not for a jury. The other thing, this was done by an expert, probably a tall man with long arms. Bardel is stocky with short limbs."

"I heard you were tricky."

"I've known Bardel for four years. He would never kill anybody: I dare say he might fiddle on expenses, but who doesn't?"

"I don't. But what do you suggest?"

"Have the inquest adjourned. It's no good going off at half-cock."

"Bardel had opportunity. He had threatened McGregor."

"To the testimony of a rather unreliable witness."

Feld smiled, "We'll see she's clean and bright on her day in court."

"No objection if I poke around, Inspector?"

"I cannot stop you!"

McGregor's Antique Shop proclaimed the fact in big, gold-painted Gothic lettering. The door to the shop was locked. So was the street door. There were five bell-pushes, with the neat brass plates underneath. Piron was hesitating in some doubt, when the door opened and a distinguished tall man with grey hair and a long thin, humorous face emerged. "Can I help you?"

"I've just come from the Inspector, sir."

"Well, don't badger me because I'm off! Here you are! Up the stairs and help yourself." Without explaining Piron slipped inside. The staircase was of beautifully carved wood, though the carpet was cheap. The late McGregor had obviously practised small economies. Miss Traylor had her apartment on the top floor, the smallest of them, Bardel had said, and in effect a one-room studio flat. Piron tapped at the door. After five minutes it opened letting out a smell compounded of dirty clothes, toasted cheese and sherry. Incongruously, she was wearing a grimy jump suit.

"I've just come from Inspector Feld," began Piron, but ceased because Miss Traylor had rotated and was walking along one wall, automatically avoiding chairs and various small tables, in the opposite direction. Upon reaching the end of the room she veered left, then left again, and eventually came back to Piron. "I asked you in," she said. "Don't be shy!" She obviously was in benevolent mood.

"Sit down!" Piron felt his buttocks pressing uncomfortably on what appeared to be fifty years of a magazine entitled *The Spiritualist.*

"At this time," said Miss Traylor, "my doctor has commanded me to take a little sherry wine to thin the blood which has a tendency to thicken. Perchance you may join."

Piron, caught in the embrace of the horrible chair—he was sure ancient slivers of toasted cheese were embedded between the magazines, gave a hopeless nod. Miss Traylor's hand was quite steady when she gave him a horrid little mustard cup filled with a fluid which had never known Andalusia, or even Australia. He wondered if she had an 'in' with some manufacturer of embalming fluid.

"My late father," said Miss Traylor, careening slightly, but settling without mishap on to a small couch of the kind Piron had never actually seen *in* anybody's house, "said a sound sherry wine was the only drink for a civilised person. Though I have been a lifelong abstainer, not wishing to give a bad example to the girls at the superior ladies' college which our family own, I felt one should abide by doctor's orders, another one of dear Father's wise sayings. Now it was about the gas stove, I think. I must say I have had very bad service and to say that the burners are clogged up with cheese is a downright lie. Cleanliness, as my father observed, is next to . . . well, a lot of things."

God, thought Piron, clutching his egg cup, she's on her third tot. "I have just seen Inspector Feld," he said.

She simpered. "That nice policeman. But why should he be interested in the drop in my pressure? But I must go and see him and explain that if there is cheese, which there is not, the company's bounden duty is to winkle it out. My doctor assures me that cheese and a little wine for my blood contain all essential nutriment."

"Did you like Mr McGregor, Miss Traylor?"

"An upstart! Dear Father would never admit Jewish girls to the finishing academy. We owned the old house when he bought it, and it was written into the Agreement, Officially Sealed in Red, that I should have the option on this flat as long as I wished, though, trust McGregor, the rent is high for my limited purse." She hiccuped.

"Loved a quarrel, didn't he, a bit of a wordy battle, like?"

"Many a wordy battle I have had with him." She chuckled. "An occasional bottle of my blood tonic dropped on his cheap old carpet! I used to tell him he was a dirty old sheeny, my father's phrase for 'em. The words he used back I would not care to repeat, though after teaching deportment to our dear girls for thirty years I was quite unshockable, as I told him."

"Nothing except a bit of fun!"

"Oh, my grandfather was Irish. Not that I like it mentioned. But there is a streak. We enjoy a good barney and no harm done."

"I'm sure you'd give as good as you got."

Miss Traylor's head was drooping and Piron said, urgently, "Anything McGregor said was fun. Anything he said was fun!"

"Yes," said Miss Traylor sleepily, and abruptly closed her eyes and began to snore.

With difficulty disgorging his buttocks from the fearful chair Piron crept to the door and let himself out.

The second apartment belonged to Mr Samuel Snegg and had two-and-a-half rooms. In himself Snegg looked like a grizzled wire-haired fox terrier. His gaze was sharp but friendly. The flat was littered with books, card indexes and files.

"I am actually representing Bardel," said Piron, seeing no point in evading it.

"Tim's all right, can't see him killing, though somebody did."

"Any idea?"

"McGregor was a fanatic record keeper; his solicitor who is his Executor asked me to take a run thorugh the books. In apple-pie order, I think, anyway the valuable stuff is intact. I went into the vault where the silver is kept and it's all there. I've checked the paintings and waters, but the small stuff I haven't yet, though you can sense atmosphere and the shop did not *feel* as though it had been rifled."

"You were employed by McGregor?" asked Piron as he took the proffered chair.

"I obliged, as the chars say. It was convenient, paid the rent and left me something over. A retired schoolmaster's pension is something to be sneezed at. I came here four years ago, and sometimes used to prowl about the shop, antique shops always being fascinating. One day McGregor approached me. He wanted somebody trustworthy when he was buying, perhaps two or three days a week. I said I knew virtually nothing, but he said I'd pick up a bit of knowledge. The prices were clearly marked, though I had authority to drop two-and-a-half per cent for cash. I enjoyed it—a good retirement for an old pedagogue."

"What was he like?"

"Odd, though of course he had foreign origins. He liked a good argy-bargy. The first day when I came in he started swearing, so I told him he could either shut up or else the deal was off. From that day he was all sweetness and light. I was never close to him, but in many ways he was a generous man. I've known him pay over the odds because the seller looked in want. What he enjoyed was a knock-down and drag-'em-out with a fellow dealer. It used to perk him up no end."

"No enemies?"

"Not in the region of his life that I knew. I suppose there are nasty characters describing themselves as dealers, but—as far as I could tell—McGregor was straight."

"Miss Traylor has it in for poor Bardel."

Snegg gave a grim little chuckle. "Miss Traylor has her ups and downs. If you can penetrate through that alcoholic fuzz you sometimes find, how shall I put it? the vestigial remnant of a fairly good brain. The family made their money out of the ladies' finishing-school business, in which you have to be fairly smart from all I've heard. I should not imagine that she would make a good witness," he added as Piron looked crest-fallen.

"If the police can get her dried out for a day or so, she could be dangerous. Juries tend to believe old ladies."

"How could they accomplish such a feat?" asked Snegg, dryly.

"A friendly police matron saying 'My dear, what about a couple of days in a nursing home at our expense to prepare yourself for the ordeal?' Once in she gets sedation and forty-eight hours' drying out plus a final shot by a doctor in Court to keep her from having the screaming shakes in the witness box."

"Could they do that?"

"Why not? They are not suborning her, merely performing a Christian duty."

"If I'm asked I'll give evidence that McGregor and Bardel were on good terms. A month ago, McGregor, who was definitely not given to compliments, said, out of nothing: 'Tim Bardel is a good fellow and we think alike!'"

"What about the other two tenants?"

"Captain Joyningstowe keeps to himself except for a cocktail party occasionally which he furbishes very well. He has an interest in the family business, is unmarried and is probably not so prosperous as he once was. A pleasant person: I doubt that he knew Bardel. McGregor was a bit in awe of him. He is a random collector and used to buy the odd, small object which caught his attention, a snuff box, a French paper-weight, that sort of thing. He has the largest flat of them all and it is very tastefully done. I gathered he used to produce a little painting, but no longer does.

"Our Miss Smith is a quaint character. Twenty-six and the daughter of a purse-proud tycoon with some kind of palatial mansion at Twickenham. Our Smith despises money, yearns for Art. Hence after four years at technical school she decamped here, getting a job at the local night school. She has some idea of setting up a small antique-cum-modern-painting shop. McGregor was amused, but he had a weakness for a pretty girl—it brought out the gallant in him—and he used to give her the run of the shop, lend her books, and occasionally embark on a ten-minute lecture. She could have done worse, one imagines. She has a weakness for unsatisfactory young men on the misunderstood-genius and can-you-lend-me-a-tenner-old-fellow side. Her latest is a rogue if I saw one, and in my profession you learned what to watch for. Thirty, I'd say, bald and bearded. The name is Jay Gould, but I gather it is just a professional name. He sells a few primitives, helps around galleries—bald-headed men with a beard and squint being notoriously sexually attractive—and when in funds takes off to the cheaper parts of Europe."

"Pot?" asked Piron.

Snegg shrugged. "Most of them use an occasional joint, as they say. Not much harm in it."

"You are being most helpful," said Piron, scribbling a note. "Was much of McGregor's business in cash?"

Snegg hesitated. "I used to do his banking on occasions. I dare say it was eighty per cent cheques or travellers' cheques—and he was a member of one of the credit-card organisations, though he was a bit careful of those. He had trading in his blood, y'know, and I think he had virtually no bad debts. Why do you ask?"

If the fox was listening you might as well flush him, thought Piron. "There are some forged notes around and, of course, it is a traffic that can breed violence."

"One can well imagine that," said Snegg, "and if McGregor had alighted upon anything it might have endangered him, but I have no knowledge of it."

"I won't keep you," said Piron, "from those indexes. Had he heirs?"

"I don't think he had any kin, but he surely made a Will, methodical as he was to the point of absurdity."

After shaking hands, Piron was on his way to the door. He had a quarter opened it when it was pushed out of his hands and a tall titian-haired girl came in.

"I'm sorry," she said quickly, "I thought it was Sneggy."

"Ah, my dear, this is Mr Piron who is investigating poor Julius' death."

(He got that in pretty smartly, thought Piron, studying her.) "Mr Piron, this is Miss June Smith."

She had the skin to go with her hair, with grey eyes flecked with green. Piron considered she was rather too buxom, but well organised and immaculately groomed.

"Please stay," she said, "there is something I wanted to consult Mr Snegg about—he's my guide, philosopher and friend, excluding my sex life."

"That's precisely where you need guidance," said Snegg, rather sourly.

The girl made no comment as she sat down, producing from her briefcase a scratch pad. Peering sideways as she reefed through it, Piron thought that he saw, broadly drawn in soft pencil, details of Regency furniture.

"Julius was giving me a lesson last Thursday," she said, "on what tell-tale things to look for in furniture. It was his scratch pad, but he said I could have it. Now look." It was a page on which, presumably, McGregor had doodled in a kind of shorthand. Snegg was peering, too.

"It is his handwriting," he said, "but the stuff itself is in his own private shorthand. He used to laugh and ask what use shorthand was if anybody else could read it."

"But there is a bit in English," the girl said, one long forefinger pointing.

'Jack Prat Query' was repeated three times.

"It looks a bit agitated," said Snegg. "His writing was usually loose and sprawling. This is cramped."

"Who is Prat?" asked Piron.

"I'll look at the customers' file," said Snegg, getting up.

When he had finished, he said "Nobody of that or similar name."

"I'd like to take this," said Piron, pulling out a pen. "I'll give you a receipt."

"No need," said Snegg. "I don't think you'll find it of any import."

The red-headed man thanked him, expressed his pleasure in meeting Miss Smith (genuine) and departed. Instead of going down the main stairs he turned left, noting that Miss Smith's flat adjoined Snegg's. At the end was a green door, obviously leading to the old servants' stairs. It was locked, but above the door was a ledge upon which rested a key.

Piron turned and gained the street. The atmosphere had been vaguely cloying and his mouth felt dry.

He would have to eat something before the journey back. Along the village street was the inevitable White Horse, probably two hundred years old but heavily restored, though well done of its kind. Piron entered it: it was too early in the evening for more than a thin spread of people to be there. It was surprisingly large. He glimpsed what was obviously a restaurant with a Victorian chop-house decor.

"Piron!" called a voice. Emerging from a door was a dapper man with a face over-running with good humour. Even as he called back, "Hallo, Alan," Piron was placing the face. A hard-working, competent manager of small hotels, frequently visited by Piron in the course of spying upon what his assistant persisted in calling 'flagrant delight'.

"I haven't seen you for two years," said Piron.

"Four," said Alan. "I scraped the money up to buy into this place. Come into the sanctum—my august presence is not required for an hour."

It was quite a room, half drawing-room, half office.

"Doing well?"

"Yes. The crack down on drunken driving made us in a way. There's Millionaire's Row a quarter of a mile away: we run the best grill room for miles. We couldn't miss. On business?"

Piron nodded.

"None of your illicit love here. We have three rooms for letting, and see to it that they are occupied permanently."

"I'm famished, Alan."

"Forgive me! A medium-rare steak sandwich and a bottle of German beer on me for old times' sake?"

"Thanks," said Piron and Alan reached for the house phone. They talked of old times until the food arrived. The sandwich was delicious and the German beer was a refreshing change from the sour fluids which Piron all too often had to quaff in his official rounds.

"I'm down here about McGregor's murder."

"It was in the stop press of the *Evening Standard*, though of course the village was full of it by noon. I never set eyes on the man: I don't think he ever came in here. I make it a point to know the locals, if only because it's worth another round if you give them the right name. But Lord! if you make a mistake! I got a good customer who I mixed up with a dog breeder. I used to say, "I see spaniels are coming back'—that kind of stuff. One night he reared back and said, 'God damn it, why do you pester me in this way?' I was astounded and told him so. He said, 'If I had my way I'd shoot the entire, bloody lot of 'em.' With that he stalked out and I've never sighted him since. The regulars told me he was a bad-tempered man in a big way of business at Kingston and used to put strychnine baits on his front lawn. Now I talk weather or racing."

"McGregor had four tenants."

The publican smiled. "I know them all. I suppose you know Miss Traylor, one of the curses of the profession—you wince when they come into sight. Not that she frequented the bars, but we've a bottle department." Alan shook his head. "We carry the usual stuff and match supermarket prices. It's a funny thing, but a lot of the rich people buy the cheaper wines if the labels look impressive enough. It's a good proportion of the turnover. Then we stock a few rock-bottom lines, including an alleged sherry. It is this—three bottles a day on average—which she buys every noon."

Piron raised his eyebrows and the publican added. "Mind you, the alcoholic content is not high, but even so . . . I did break my rule and talk to the old soul occasionally. The family came from here, but ran a school in Switzerland. I happen to know Switzerland a bit, so we have a little in common.

"Then, of course, there's old Joyningstowe. He has a little circle of friends here. He's the last of an old, decayed family type. Unless you knew that his lineage is impeccable and that he was a permanent army officer you might think him too good to be true.

"Snegg is my favourite Scotch terrier. He taught maths at the secondary school and his former pupils often collar him and bring him along with the intention of getting him drunk. Not that they succeed, because he's a hard-headed Scot and after four whiskies shuts up shop. But I envy him his popularity."

"There's a girl, June Smith."

"The Technical College lot. Harmless, at the age when it's all talk, talk, and reforming things. Everything from Women's Lib to Mao via art terms I don't quite grasp. Wants her arse smacked, does Miss Smith, but a very nice girl at that. They say her father is rolling in the lolly."

"Doesn't she have a boy friend?"

"My word, you've a nose." said Alan admiringly. "He calls himself Jay Gould."

"What is he like?"

"Flamboyant and when you get close to him he's much bigger than he looks in the distance. Say six feet two, big face, attractive enough, but if you look closely his eyes are cold and nasty and the mouth is too thin. Blond, balding hair, as per schedule. The funny thing is that seven years ago—which would make him around twenty-five—I got caught for jury service, six horrible days of it. He went under the name of Chining and was one of six defendants in a misrepresentation case concerning two thousand pounds' worth of Oriental carpets. Chining was the expert who certified them. They were worth about three hundred pounds, and came from Germany. It was a muddled old business, purposely so no doubt, with damn all in writing that mattered. We didn't convict: they had refunded the money. Afterwards the officer in charge of the jury told us over a drink that the police knew them as a shady lot. I gathered they weren't violent or anything of that nature, but always ready to seize the main chance."

"Do you know what he does?"

"He paints. Somebody told me that he is talented, but it's a crowded market. He deals a bit, manages the odd fill-in job at a gallery. He is a bit of a hero type to the young fry, seems to have travelled a fair amount. A name-dropper, of course, but he makes pretty certain nobody knows the person in question."

It had been an evil drive against the traffic to Piron's Central London flat. He arrived at a little before nine, and was disposed to have a bowl of soup and an evening catching up with his reading. However he showered and at ten was in one of his clubs, a gloomy relic of the nineteen hundreds which still provided excellent service from its elderly waiters and good plain food. Quite a few of its members were civil servants and policemen. Piron was lucky, for the Inspector he had hoped for had finished his nightly game of chess and was seated in his accustomed chair at a bow window overlooking a disused cemetery, in actual fact a romantic sight upon a moonlit evening.

Piron had a liking for the elderly bachelor, soon due for retirement, and ordered two Scotches. Presently he said, "Do you know a Jack Prat, Alf?" The Inspector had always been a desk man, fortified by the phenomenal memory possessed by some C.I.D. officers. After a time he said, "I fancy it is Prah! Jack Prat! If it is the one, he is a gambler. Oh, no, not crooked. He plays bridge better than ninety-eight per cent of the population and poker ditto. He doesn't cheat: he doesn't have to because he's got the percentage. People, wealthy people, like a good game. Prat's aim is to win, say, twenty-five pounds an evening. For five months he goes to the States. There are bridge tournaments there with much kudos for the winners. He's a professional partner: it's quite legitimate, with liberal expenses and a fee. Plus I expect a few deals on the side. He probably makes from this about sixteen thousand a year. The Inland Revenue tax him on three thousand a year, from investments. He likes the good things, is very charming, and has the entrée to some quite distinguished circles."

"Yet you know him?"

"His name often crops up. There's an international syndicate that fixes a few sporting events each year. They keep it on the conservative side, not wanting to kill the goose. Prat is reportedly their English agent, just overseeing and getting the betting side fixed. He was on my file three years ago. A young Canadian was over here. He had unexpectedly inherited three hundred thousand dollars, so he came over here to get into business. When his solicitor brought him into my office he had three hundred dollars. Nothing we could do—he'd bought a dud company. His first acquaintance in London was a charming bloke named Jack Prat."

The Inspector scooped up potato crisps. "The funny thing was that he had nothing against Prat, who in fact had recommended him to an accountant, a bogus one who subsequently was convicted for three months on a quite different matter. What had happened, so an informer told us, was that Prat put the young fellow on the auction block, selling him to a gang of con-men for six thousand pounds. He does that: if he finds a situation to be exploited he'll put it out for sale. Naturally, he doesn't touch the dirty work himself."

"A nice fellow!"

"There are scores of them, Piron. They rarely go inside except when they yield to some foolish impulse. The last one I remember was grossing fifteen thousand a year when he stole a top coat out of a restaurant—we managed to get him eleven months inside. Anyway what have you got on him?"

"There was an antique dealer at Frippingham killed today. He apparently knew Prat, but had some reservations. It's pretty tenuous, but there's a whiff of forgery which tickles my nose. The local Inspector is not a co-operative type: refers to me as a private eye. He wants to nab Bardel—you know him."

"Yes," the Inspector scratched his chin and ordered another. "Feld—that's the man you refer to?"

"Yes."

"He's a good copper, with no imagination, but he'll end up as a Super, never fear. However, I read about the case in the afternoon file. We aren't in on it, but I'll see a few enquiries are made, though Prat does not strike me as a killer, but as I said before they have silly impulses. You scratch my back and I'll attend to yours."

II

MR HOGG, PIRON'S pimply, youthful assistant, was in a eupeptic and annoying frame of mind next morning, and insisted on playing back a somewhat remarkable tape of conversation between an Alderman and his lady typist, the Agency having been fee'd by Mrs Alderwoman.

"He seems to be gilding the lily," said Piron, patiently.

"Green plastic paint," leered Hogg.

"A figure of speech."

Hogg guffawed. "I must tell that in the local. She's got a smashing figure, but as to the speech part she is a bit dumb. 'Yes Your Honour', and so forth. However, she'll do very well, him being a wealthy man."

"Get the report to the solicitor," said Piron. "Make it quick, say three-quarters of an hour. I have telephone calls to make."

There were times, though not too often, when Piron wished he were back in his native New York. This morning he did. The British were a bit hard to understand and their own particular brand of evasion was not to Piron's early morning taste. His friend at the Yard provided Jack Prat's address, a chi-chi apartment block. Prat was not on the telephone: "He uses call boxes," said his informant.

It took him thirty-five minutes to get his favourite free-lance woman operative in. She was fiftyish, handsome and charming: women let their hair down to her and sometimes served as much as seven years as the result. Piron handed her a quarto sheet. "A Miss Traylor, aged seventy, intelligent and given to plonk. A lush. You know Tim Bardel, of course. This lady may try to swear against him. The Inquest is at twelve tomorrow. The Inspector is a cutie. He'll get her in the hands of a police matron —a free check-up for her nerves and dry her out. At ten o'clock you get into her flat, on a public opinion poll, with a bottle of brandy in your briefcase."

"I don't like it, Piron!"

"Expenses plus forty."

"Forty-five," she parried. Piron nodded.

"Done, but only because of Tim Bardel."

"It's your great big heart, dearie. I want her so pissed she doesn't know Arthur from Martha," said Piron.

"Nothing more, Piron?"

"You don't know a Jack Prat?"

"Only as an operator. He's known among the smart boys and girls. An international practice, they say. A Clever One. He runs parties and a friend of mine provides the girls, high-class whores who you'd never pick. I heard he had an interest in a casino, but it's very discreet. I'd stay out of that one, Piron."

"Thanks, May. You might get down there tonight. There's quite a decent pub named the White Horse. They don't let rooms, but I've scribbled a line to the proprietor, a friend of mine, and he'll see you get a bed, either there or in the village."

She looked at the name on the envelope. "Alan! I've known him off and on these twenty years. He's co-operative to a point: used to quip that if people had to commit adultery they could not complain of being peered at through keyholes."

"Here's thirty quid on account." The red-headed detective peeled off notes. "And don't forget I want the old party speechless."

"A doctor friend will give me a little something—quite harmless—to add to the brew."

"I admire you your strong head, May!"

"Be your age, Piron, I use a trick briefcase. There are two bottles, one coloured water. I did have a friend who became very bad when she got the two mixed up."

No sooner had she gone than Hogg came in holding a purloined letter, the property of the lecherous Alderman, which he described as very tasty.

"I don't want to hear it," said Piron irritably. "It's Tim Bardel, he's in trouble."

"I thought his wife kept him that busy that he had no time . . ."

"It's murder, Hogg. Shut that acne trap and listen."

In spite of his unsavoury appearance, Hogg possessed a great deal of Cockney shrewdness. "I don't see Tim, crafty though he is, doin' anybody in," he said as he worked on his nose, "and as far as this Prat is concerned, that type put the work out to contract by pros. I never took much interest, not being our line of country, but over where I live it's gettin' fashionable, millionaires going in for the arty-crafty and boutiques. I did hear some talk about fakes. Apparently in the twenties it was the Yanks who was the suckers, but now they got this credibility gap, and it's us who are the marks."

"Facts!"

"Now, guv, what facts are there? I tell you it's a fifteenth-century porringer, a pot as far as I know, and it's mildly hot at three hundred nicker. You're happy, the wife top-notes it at her parties." Hogg assumed the hideous falsetto which he apparently imagined was the trade mark of the fair sex, " 'Ave you seen our old porringer? Six 'undred nicker it cost my hubby and the hexperts say it was a steal. But Alf always has a wonderful nose for a bargain, like when 'e got me like, the ruffian. We thought we'd pick up a set of them for punch bowls, now 'e's doin' so well exporting French letters to our Common Markit friends."

Hogg rolled his eyes. "Afterwards the other ladies tell their husbands they must collect something. They say there's a bloke who makes Spanish silver coins recovered from the Armada. Fifty pence it costs him in silver and labour, and he flogs 'em at five notes each. No, Mr Pee, there are no rules to that game, and if you work it out the suckers have a vested interest in keeping quiet."

"The honest dealers don't like it."

Hogg was trying to scratch between his shoulder blades. "Honest people never do like it," he said, "and that's how people like us make a crust. I sometimes wake up sweatin' 'cause I dreamed everybody had turned honest overnight and you and I were on the end of a pick on the roads."

"I told Tim to keep close to home," said Piron, "but to pick up anything he could by telephone. You might drop out to see him."

His personal telephone rang. It was Milly Bardel, a generally unflappable woman.

"I'm worried about Tim, Mr Piron. He got up at six, his usual hour, and said he had a call to make but would be back for coffee and toast at eight thirty. He is not home."

"He could have been delayed."

"It's just a feeling I have," she said uneasily. "Oh, Tim told me all about the murder and how the fools suspected him. But if he says he'll be home at a certain hour, well he always is, without fail."

"Hogg will be out," said Piron as reassuringly as he could.

"Probably been given a bashing," said Hogg after Piron had recounted the conversation. "Might be connected with this case, or might not. Bardel was never frightened about sticking his bib in. I'll go out and do the necessary."

"I'll visit Mr Jack Prat," said Piron.

"You want your head read, guv," said his underling.

In the event Piron was almost embarrassed by the weight of the small cosh clipped to his left armpit: Jack Prat, who answered the door of the fifteen-thousand-pound apartment—by Piron's estimate—was as affable as he was well groomed. A trim six feet one, with iron-grey curly hair, his genial smile must have been worth half his income.

"Come in and forgive the mess," he said after Piron had explained his business. "I contract the cleaning out and they don't turn up for half an hour."

There was little mess, at any rate in the large film-set type of room redolent of expensive cologne, good cigars and whisky. It was all a trifle larger than life. Prat arranged his long limbs in studied, elegant disarray. "I like going from A to Z, Mr Piron. First, I gather you know about me?"

"Report is that you are an honest pro gambler."

"Fair enough. It is hardish work and the Income Tax don't like you, because gambling is not respectable, though the stock market is. One way and the other I have funds in this country that I'd like to put into things, having looked at auction reports over the years. Diamonds I mistrust, because of the 'bleed' from Sierra Leone. I thought of pictures and metal objects. In fact I have quite a bit put by for the purpose. A year ago I started from scratch, reading the books, meeting the dealers, and along the line I met McGregor, a dedicated dealer, perhaps on the grabbing-your-lapel-and-pulling-you-into-the-shop side. But his reputation was good. Six weeks ago he sat where you are and told me that he was commissioned to sell two hundred thousand pounds' worth of old silver for one hundred and fifty thousand: payment, cash within six months."

Prat got up and helped himself to a weak whisky-and-water from the bar in the corner. "Join me?"

"Too early," said Piron.

"He said that somebody with the same idea of things as myself had been discreetly buying for six years. Whoever it was had got into a hole and had to liquidate. Public auction was impossible because it would destroy his credit rating, and, I suspected, alert our taxation friends. I told him that I couldn't finance a deal of that magnitude, but that I might promote a syndicate. Of course we would want all the expert opinion going."

"What was in it for him?"

"Three per cent from the seller," said Prat. "He was quite frank about it. The upshot was that I raised three partners. McGregor was providing an English assessor, I got in touch with a good man from Brussels and my associates had a Swiss."

"There were meetings?"

"I conducted the negotiations by telephone. There would be one meeting at a designated place, with solicitors to draw up the agreement."

"Sounds a good set-up for a confidence show."

"Even if you count me out, my friends do not confide easily." There was a hint of brutality under Prat's lazy smile.

"Of course." In the background was the sound of a vacuum cleaner turned on. "Where was the meeting to be?"

"Water under the bridge, I'm much afraid I can't add anything more. Should McGregor's principal get in touch with me, then we will go on with it. No, I don't know the name, McGregor being that cagey. I must say that I do not believe that his death had any connection with this matter."

"I'm not at all suggesting that its genesis lay in the area of your discussions with him, but it is a valuable collection and where there's money there may be murder. One thing, who introduced you to McGregor? I mean there must have been a moment when a bod said 'Mr Prat I'd like you to meet Mr McGregor, an officer and a gentleman'."

Even when his face went blank, as it did then, an aura of geniality seemed to cover Prat like the patina of a Grecian vase. "Let me see! I remember a Chelsea exhibition. It was a youngish man named Jay Gould."

"Do you know him well?"

Prat chuckled. "You know the young man who is on the edge of the party, trying to hog the potato chips, and snatch a new sherry as it is being passed. Not quite that: he can talk and I'm told that he himself does reasonable abstracts, but a little out of it. I know people, you must if you are a gambler, and I would say he was insecure and perhaps a little bit crooked. Now, if you'll excuse me, I've got to pay the cleaners and then go out."

The Bardels lived in North London, in an old house prudently purchased in the late fifties and smelling of stewed chicken, upon which the family lived. When Piron got there the door opened six inches to his ring and he glimpsed Mr Hogg holding a steel multiple wrench.

Mercifully the children had their lunches at school, or in canteens, so the big living-room was dominated by the couch upon which a bandaged Bardel lay, fussed over by a surprisingly svelte wife.

"I didn't altogether take your advice," said Bardel. "This morning I went out early and was collared at the corner—I was on foot—and given the treatment. Ten minutes of it. I can't walk for maybe three or four days, that's all. But it will look fine at the Inquest when I'm wheeled in. I got the notice half an hour ago."

Piron looked at him clinically. He had two spectacular black eyes, which made his face look horrible, but the main damage was the skilled application of steel-shod boots to his ankles and feet.

"Did you get a medical certificate?"

"That and pain killers, but it will look like hell."

"Who did it?"

"Three young pros. Two held me while the third bashed. I'll be right and about in a fortnight—there's nothing broken. However I look like a man of violence: I can just imagine the jurymen peering at me."

"We'll get you down there by ambulance," said Piron. "Hogg, will you get on to our solicitor? We'd better get down there to represent Tim. I suppose Feld will appear for the police. I'll try to see him before. What we want is a three-week adjournment."

Bardel adjusted himself upon the sofa. "You don't suppose that Feld will pass up the opportunity for getting that old crone Traylor's testimony well and truly on the record!"

"We'll see. Now Tim, what did the three look like?"

"I didn't see, only feel, the two who held me, but the one who used his boots and fists was around five feet ten, brown hair, fresh complexioned, nattily dressed. His face is fish-like, something about the nose I think. Hard green eyes."

"There was a cove pointed out to me out Islington way," muttered Hogg, "and it could be him. Name of Sparrow or Swallow or something, but known as the Dickybird. Comes of a whole family of wrong 'uns. The Dickybird is a cut above his brothers—knows how to use a fish knife. A high class 'minder' around the big gambling set: not much work, but when it does come it can be fierce."

"Brainy?" asked Piron.

"Very crafty, I was told. He went to Approved School, then Borstal, and at eighteen went in for carving somebody up. A

Head spotted him as a likely lad and took him up when he came out. Wot a life!"

"How many people did you get in touch with yesterday?" Piron demanded of Bardel, who looked acutely embarrassed.

"I phoned maybe twenty people, say five minutes each, all in the antique world. I told them that McGregor had been killed, with me discovering him. I asked if they had seen him recently."

Piron said in disgust, "It would have been all over London."

"I was casting groundbait," protested Bardel.

"You made yourself the bait," said Piron, "and there was some quite fancy thinking. Teach you a lesson against sticking your snout in, and prejudicing the case by having you look like a broken-down thug. I'd keep the front door locked, but it's a remote chance that anybody's going to bother you again."

"The police said they'd keep an eye on the house," said Mrs Bardel. "I phoned up the desk sergeant whose wife I know."

"Easy to see that the brains are kept in the kitchen!" said Piron. "Keep him quiet and away from the phone."

It was a reluctant Hogg that led Piron to a friend in Islington, a greasy little fellow who ran a small wholesale novelty warehouse currently featuring a smashing line of plastic chastity belts and little boxes of itching powder. 'All the Fun for the Fair', his notices proclaimed.

"Dickybird," he said after Piron had given him ten pounds. "Nobody wants to mess with him."

Piron's long bony fingers prized painfully into his shoulders. "I want to mess with him a trifle."

"You'd keep me right out?"

"Right back in the itching powder."

"He lives up Runting Street in a new blocker flats called 'Owie Court. In just fifteen minutes' time he comes out and walks to a liddle private club he's interested in. He has a bite there and sees people."

Piron gave him a long look. "Start phoning, brother, and I'll fix your ears in a chastity belt."

It was nice to regain what passed for fresh air in Islington.

"Nice friends you seem to meet," he told Hogg.

"You meet all kinds in this game, Mr Pee."

"Only thing is yours are gamier than most." Piron caught the eye of a passing cab driver.

"What's Runting Street like?" he asked as they drove away.

"Small flats, some studio. Everybody out to work all day."

It was a short five-minute haul, as the cabbie was at pains to point out, being slightly mollified when Piron over-tipped.

"Howie Court is that greenhouse-looking place at the top. It's a cul-de-sac. Used to be a proper thieves' kitchen years ago, so I was once told."

Now it was one of the featureless 'new' streets, shopless, apart from a small supermarket at the end, and at this hour bereft of people. Sure enough, as they walked along a man emerged from Howie Court. Piron judged his suit would be cheap at a hundred guineas: a theatrical tailoring job, hand sewn. As they got nearer, Piron took a swift look at the feet. They were ensconced in soft antelope, the Dickybird having dispensed with working attire. They were about to pass him when Piron swiftly moved left, bringing one foot down heavily on Dickybird's instep. The fish face remained impassive, only the eyes flickering. Piron had time to notice the signs of incipient baldness: in a few years the man would look fishy indeed.

"Look where you're going," he said mildly enough, even as one hand flashed in his pocket.

Piron chopped his long nose with his right hand, stiffened his left fingers and prodded the man's stomach. The Dickybird knew enough to go down on his hams.

"Name of Piron! You leave my boys alone." The red-headed man stood back.

After the Dickybird had finished being sick, he said, "I'll remember you."

"That's what I want, punk."

From the corner of his eye, Piron saw two middle-aged ladies across the road. They averted their gaze. It was obviously that kind of district.

They left the Dickybird shakily getting to his feet.

"Was that necessary, guv?" asked Hogg nervously.

"You learned a lesson, boy. At the Agency we don't strong-arm anyone. However what happens if 'they' beat up an operative is that the thug in question gets something he remembers."

"You could go to the police."

"The thug's employer gets the best legal talent. It drags on. Finally it costs a great deal of money, Mr Thug is fined five dollars with a three-month suspended sentence. He's back on the job next day."

"I didn't like the way the Dickybird looked at you."

"How the hell should a thug look? We'll get a cab back. Fix up about Bardel's appearance, then stick your nose into immorality for the rest of the day."

Next morning Piron, driving his nondescript car, picked up the Agency's solicitor (who if consulted would have preferred his own chauffeured Jensen).

"This old bottled trout Traylor sounds dangerous," he said after Piron had talked at length.

"It will have to be kid gloves and the polite suggestion of genteel senility."

He parked in the yard of Frippingham Police Station. "'Ere!" said the custodian.

"Officer of the Court to see Inspector Feld," snapped Piron, and while the man was digesting this fact, led the way in through the back entrance which smelled of years of disinfecting. They went along an aisle between the six cells that the station possessed, now empty, the doors open to display the pail and other dismal comforts within. The desk sergeant looked at them rather askance until the solicitor produced his card. "Representing one Timothy Bardel, to see Inspector Feld."

"Ah," said the Sergeant, jerking his thumb towards a double door, "the Boss is in Reception."

Piron pushed open the swing doors and they walked through. The Inspector was looking drearily at Miss Traylor who, partially supported by a harassed-looking policewoman, was surveying the little world with a bleary smile.

"I left her at eight thirty," the policewoman was protesting, "as sober as my mother."

The Inspector's glare impaled her and by inference her mother.

It was in fact Miss Traylor who saw Piron first.

"I haven't seen you for yearsh," she said, friskily, "are you still teaching the ski-ing sheniors?" Hand tremulously outstretched she tried to stand but could not make it.

"Take her home," said Feld quietly.

The policewoman half carried her through the doors, and the Inspector's dyspeptic glance turned to Piron. "You heard it!" He said bitterly. "As full as a boot." He saw the solicitor. "Who is this?"

"My name is Birdly, and I represent Mr Bardel."

"He's here?"

"An ambulance case. If you insist on calling him, it will mean a wheelchair. He was attacked in the street yesterday."

"Brawling, eh?"

"It was a professional job: two held him, one put the boot in."

"Are you alleging it has to do with the murder?"

"I'm alleging nothing. You have a drunken witness who cannot appear, I have a sober man in a wheelchair. What say, medical evidence and a month's adjournment?"

The Inspector's stomach rumbled. It was a sure sign they had gained their point, realised Piron.

"We have the Pathologist," said Feld. "Will you cross-examine?"

"Two questions only," said Birdly.

"You won't renege?"

"I'll overlook the question because you are obviously tired."

"Sorry, I suppose I am." He looked at Piron. "Is there anything to these hints of yours?"

"I think McGregor was a victim of part curiosity, part righteousness, a bad combination. There seems to be a lot of forging in the way of old silver. It might be that somebody stopped his mouth. Again, he was currently the agent in a large antique deal by private treaty to one Jack Prat—pronounced Prah—who is a wheeler-dealer."

"Prat?" Feld was a good policeman, thought Piron, as the Inspector, tired as he was, flipped through his memory banks. "There was a mention some time back in the weekly digest. Let's see, is he interested in a casino?"

"I believe so. Personally he is a straight gambler, not a mechanic, but a gentleman who would sell you straight down the river for fifty quid."

The police, as the sharp little Coroner ascertained, had first viewed deceased at eight thirty-three a.m. The Pathologist, questioned by Mr Birdly, opined that on evidence McGregor could have been dead by six, though he thought that somewhere after seven thirty would be nearer. The weapon was probably a knife discovered in the shop.

Mr Birdly: "Would the killer be suffused with blood?"

Reply: "Not necessarily. Deceased had poor circulation, but there was extensive bleeding though not, if I may use the phrase, spurting. This could imply medical knowledge on the part of the killer."

"And he would be long-armed and right-handed?"

"It appeared to be a back-handed stroke. But I must say that I did not anticipate this point. Perhaps . . ."

The Coroner interposed: "I gather all concerned are agreeable to a month's adjournment."

And so it was settled.

Outside the Court, an extension of that used by the Magistrates, Bardel waited in his ambulance, flanked by his folding wheelchair and three attendants. They were playing solo.

"Adjourned for a month," said Piron, peering into the smoke-filled interior.

"This expense will break me," said Bardel.

"You're three quid up on the game," said the head attendant.

"We'll worry about that later," said Piron.

"My old woman will worry *me* tonight when she goes through my pockets," mourned one of the attendants, "though how she thinks I can get a woman for twelve and six passes the imagination."

"There's always the Common Market," said Piron. "No trouble, Tim?"

"A constable was around the house the whole mortal night: the wife kept clambering out of bed and peering through the windows."

"I would not think that Bardel is in much jeopardy," said the solicitor as they walked away. "I suppose we'd better have lunch here. I've got an appointment at four thirty."

The village possessed the usual Tudor restaurant: at its well raftered entrance, Piron felt a tap on his shoulder. He had to think for a minute.

"Saw you going into McGregor's t'other day as I was coming out. The police, you said. I'm Captain Joyningstowe."

Little lies always caught up with you, thought Piron. "I came from the Police Inspector, as representing a party involved in the case."

"I quite often eat here," said the Captain. "I get the two thirty into town."

"This is Mr Birdly. We could share a table and give you a lift up."

"Good English food," the Captain led the way past a couple of smiling waitresses, "but avoid anything else. They have to turn on fancy stuff for the long-haired ones from London."

The soup was tinned tomato, but the mixed grill was first class, and they relaxed over it. "Do you go to London every day, sir?" asked Piron.

"Most days I make myself a nuisance around the shop. Something to do. An old widower like me gets bored, and music can't fill your whole life. I envied McGregor in a way, because he lived entirely for his work. I never have possessed a dilettante strain."

"Did you like McGregor?"

"Like?" Joyningstowe sounded genuinely astounded. "One doesn't like or dislike a fellow of that ilk! He was polite to me: that was all I required. He was a kind of barrow boy in a shop. Knew his stuff, I think. I bought a few bits and pieces there. No bargains, but fair enough. I know a little of antiques, the family having had this book business, and McGregor was sound enough . . ."

A buxom waitress came round and they ordered the apple pudding.

"You were saying?"

"That with all his expertise McGregor might be easy prey to a dishonest practitioner. He was self-centred and thought he knew everything. At the bookshop we're not above taking a second opinion, or even a third: but McGregor made up his mind with a snap. In my somewhat limited experience such men can be imposed upon, but it is, was, none of my business. The Turkish coffee here is not bad, by the way. I do know dealers, through the book trade, and I just got the feeling that McGregor, though dedicated, was gullible."

"He bought himself, so I understand, not through an agent."

"There's a man named Snegg. A retired pedagogue. He is a smooth customer. I would not altogether trust him. He was in McGregor's confidence, there is absolutely no doubt of that. I don't want to set myself up as a mischief-maker, but Snegg has had financial difficulties. There is a nephew who he backed in a small way of business. He came a cropper."

Piron waited until the coffee stage. "Did you know Timothy Bardel?"

"I think McGregor introduced us once. Sharp-looking fellow, but courteous. But I hardly saw anything of him. A lot of regulars used to frequent the store—quite a clublike atmosphere in a way.

I sometimes glimpsed Bardel. He rather gave me the impression that he minded his own business."

"I suppose you know Jay Gould?"

"June Smith's latest! Have you met her?"

"Yes."

"We are all in an avuncular position, except I suppose poor old Traylor is an auntie. She has an appalling taste in men. Gould is the bottom of the barrel, though it's only my opinion. Trouble is"—he gave an attractive grin—"I'm an old Army type rooted in the hairless era, so you must thus discount me. I'm touching seventy—and for God's sake don't say 'you don't look it', because I take pains not to—and what opinions I have are scandalous to this generation. But I do think Jay Gould would be improved by six months in a fairly tough prison."

"It would seem to be a rising opinion that the human race, or its young, should all be in tough prisons," said Piron. "But who would work the coal mines, which are the same?"

Joyningstowe guffawed. "I remember being pushed about in the Army and resenting it. Don't place me as an embalmed old fool, just have a clinical look at Gould. Probably what annoys me most is that he is so physically clean: shampoos the long locks, stinks of cologne, cuts and colours his goddam toenails. In my day they were just plain dirty. I should be dead, but I enjoy living."

Piron, over some protest from the Captain, paid for the meal.

Joyningstowe slumbered, lightly, in the back seat before they dropped him at Knightsbridge, where he had some business.

Birdly had largely been silent. Now he said: "An odd crowd of witnesses, Piron. A Prosecutor's nightmare, I should think. Joyningstowe is an old gossip, I guess."

It was not quite what you knew, but who. Piron checked the company car into the garage and took his own to see a scar-faced man who walked with his eyes down so that he did not arouse sleeping dogs. His name was Harold, but Piron thought of him as a perambulatory dogs' home. Virtually no act of violence in southern England had taken place over thirty years without Harold having cognisance and perhaps profit. His origins were obscure, and his soupy voice revealed little. He was wealthy and unhappy. At one time he had got into trouble in New York, brash outside his territory, and the Agency had extricated him, for which a certain debt remained, not financial but arising from the fact that the Agency had found out a great deal about him.

He lived luxuriously but cheerlessly with a skinny wife who perpetually complained of the cost of living. You were never invited to sit down. Eyeing Piron, he scuffed his foot into the Axminster.

"Fellow named McGregor got hit," said Piron. "Was it contracted?"

Although looking perpetually about to scratch Harold got a point quickly. "A shop-keeper," he said, " 'ence a hamateur job. Cove is in 'is shop, surprises the boy and it 'appens. The curse of the profession, as you right well know. No, there was no contrack out concernin' one McGregor. I never heard of 'im, in fack."

"What about Jack Prat?"

The Axminster stood up like cat's fur as Harold slid his feet.

"You don't want to meddle with Jack Prat, though I have set up a coupla jobs for 'im. Smooth like Mum's treacle tart, arsenic underneath. But nobody was 'ired to hit this McGregor, take me oath on it."

"You might keep your ears open."

"My effin' ears extend to the Isle a' Wight," said Harold, "without straining 'em furder. Take it from me, it was an amateur job."

Enough was enough, and Piron was glad to quit Harold.

The day's mail had included an invitation to the opening of a gallery. The first show was reputed to be important, though ordinarily he would probably not have gone. Such affairs often yielded gossip, and sometimes you could note who was newly sleeping with whom, a circumstance often professionally of interest to Piron. He went home and changed.

He walked in to the smell of cigar smoke and expensive scent and greeted his host, whose two divorces the Agency had discreetly handled. He was harassed but had the knack of appearing to give unlimited attention to each new guest. Piron did not keep him, but wandered into a corner where there was strange sculpture with holes in it. He appeared to be engrossed. From the corner of his eye he saw Captain Joyningstowe doing the old-school act with a couple of stern dowagers, and—he nearly whistled—near him was Jack Prat, tuxedoed, urbane and apparently engrossed in a catalogue. Talking to him was June Smith, with a youngish man in a white suit. There was a slightly foppish air about him. On sight Piron was prepared to dislike him.

"One can only say that there is a certain fascination . . ." said a voice beside him. It was Mr Snegg in rusty black.

"You mean the art or the people?"

"Probably both, but no coincidence about the people from the flats. We all had invitations, and I shared a taxi with June Smith and her boy friend, an extravagance, but then the Executors are paying me to carry on *pro tem.*, so one supposes it will come off income tax."

"Did McGregor leave a Will?"

"I found one among his papers: drawn up in London fifteen years ago when his mother died. There are a few codicils—two hundred pounds to me among others, though I suppose he might have envisaged that I should be a stop-gap, but the bulk is to Jewish charities. The shop will be sold, but it might take six months, it being so specialised."

"The boy friend is the rather flashy article?" Piron glanced across the room.

"The same old Jay Gould. I incline to think that he needs a psychiatrist."

"And the groomed man with him?"

"Looking at him makes me feel shabby," mourned Snegg. "I gathered his name was Prat. His face is familiar, but those tall, well groomed men tend to look a little alike."

"I see the sherry, a reasonable brand, is being circulated," said Piron, "and I should like to meet Mr Gould."

The red-headed man towered over everybody except Jack Prat who, however, had imbedded himself in the crowd around.

"Didn't know you were coming, Mr Piron," said Joyningstowe. "Odd collection, interesting but out of touch with me."

"You being strictly representational," said Gould.

"Do you know Mr Gould?" asked Joyningstowe, unperturbed. "I think a rose is a rose: he thinks it looks like an aborted cabbage." He performed the introduction.

"You are a private eye?" Gould obviously had the trick of being offensive in an inoffensive manner.

Piron mentioned the Agency and had some satisfaction in seeing recognition in Gould's rather protuberant eyes. It meant nothing: the Agency was frequently written about.

"An American, of course?"

"Fugitive from the draft!"

"Up to the sixty-year-olds, are they?" said Gould. "My word, who will star in the films?"

"They are not calling up the women, it being inhumane to the various enemies."

"Now littlies," said June Smith, "peace is wonderful, etcetera."

She had a certain panache which glowed, Piron thought, in company, and she looked quite beautiful.

"Did you not introduce Mr Prat to McGregor?" He was a punk, thought Piron.

"Jack?" Gould raised his bushy eyebrows—he had all the facial tricks. "He gets around. He's interested in old silver, so I might have introduced them. Julius had taken to going to affairs like this. In his riper years I think he was getting McGregarious."

Piron had an urge to punch him in the mouth.

"I think I'd like to go home soon," said June Smith.

"Nonsense," said Gould, masterfully, "what you need is a change of air."

He guided her away, and Piron accepted a sherry from a hovering and interested waiter.

"They are very strange today," said Joyningstowe. "I have observed that young man among violent-looking company. Funny how it alters from generation to generation. When I was a boy it was razors, cut-throats, then safety razor blades. We had the bit with bicycle chains and Edwardian dress. Now it's boots, knives and the occasional gun."

"I would not like to have lived in 1780," said Mr Snegg, collaring a passing egg with mayonnaise. "They used to immerse passers-by in boiling water."

"Tastes change," said the Captain. "They used to like flagellation then. I have often wondered what it was like. Now the politicos and trades unions flagellate you mentally, less interesting one imagines."

"When I started," said Mr Snegg, "there was no difficulty in getting student teachers because they could use the rod. Some of the old fellows used practically to be sustained by the thought."

"A thrashing does no boy any harm," said the Captain.

"Perhaps you'll excuse me, there's a fellow over there . . ." said Piron.

Jack Prat, watching Piron working his way through the throng, evidently became resigned to the encounter, though his pale blue eyes belied his customary smile. Piron thought that smiling became obsessive.

"Do these things attract you?" asked Prat casually.

"Part of my job. I go to meetings intent on preserving otters. Once it was an old lady on about vipers—very good champagne she served. You see odd people, sometimes useful."

Prat grinned. "I, too, collect people. I live by a modest percentage, but I don't like *being* collected."

"People have tried hard to collect me, Mr Prat. I just run too fast."

"But I never run, Piron!"

Somebody might have played tricks with the central heating, but the room was getting hot. Piron noted a sweat drop at the side of Prat's Roman nose.

"We should play it cool," said Piron.

"Trouble is that I do not know what you want."

"I do not want Timothy Bardel arraigned for murder."

"I don't see that I can help."

"Let's lay the cards on the table, Mr Prat."

Prat grinned. "You talk like a riverboat gambler, Piron. They used to shoot men for less along Ol' Miss'."

"You have the rep of playing it straight"—Piron returned grin for grin—"and there has been a rumour concerning counterfeiting."

"Old Masters." Prat sounded amused.

"Among other things, currency."

"That's a dicey business," said Prat. "I thought it had not been a big operation for years owing to the difficulty in passing notes. When they are used it is in connection with a con trick, stage money kind of stuff. In the gambling business there is nothing of that sort. Try to pass the snide in a casino, and, oh, brother!"

"It's just that McGregor's name was floating about in connection with it."

"I find it difficult to believe," said Prat slowly. "He was an honest little fellow always chasing a buck. He told me he came up the hard way selling surplus warehouse stock off a barrow."

"If you should hear of anything," said Piron moving away.

"Sure," said Prat with practised insincerity.

June Smith was on what probably was her fourth sherry and looked it. She was studying a composition of straight lines, ignoring Jay Gould. Gould shrugged and moved away.

"Do I sense non-enjoyment?" said Piron softly.

"This damned murder. I liked McGregor, and to regard his murder as a personal nuisance is something abominable. But I do: life has seemed an absolute misery since he was found dead. Even people look different and I don't like opening the door of my flat."

"We'd better get going," said Piron, "worry and a sherry diet tends to make you fall flat on your face: besides which the sausage rolls look sinister."

There was a bowl of iced soup and some thick-cut ham in the

refrigerator of Piron's small apartment and they ate that and listened to tapes for a couple of hours.

Then: "Who murdered Julius, Piron?"

"I think a forger, my dear. It seems to add up to that, though there is some niggling in my mind."

"You can rule out poor old Traylor . . . I suppose you heard that she turned up to the Inquest reeling? I know the Inspector, or more so his wife—they are both quite nice. That leaves me—and what motive can I have? I might as well tell you that disliking me as he does, my father dislikes death duties more, and I shall not starve. Snegg? A pleasant old bumbler. Joyningstowe—from the nineteen thirties, a gentleman tosspot."

"Your boy friend?"

"Ex. A casualty of the last two days. He was what the last generation called a spiv, but with talents, though Christ knows there is so much current talent."

"What was his relationship with McGregor?"

"Oh, Jay, gets on with people well." She wriggled her bare feet. "Though, paradoxically, people don't like him. I rather like people who aren't liked."

"It seems unnecessary, it's easy to be liked."

"You mistake it personally for people being afraid of you."

She had moved closer to him.

"Better get you home or to a hotel if you are nervous."

"It's not quite that. I do not see why anybody should kill me. I know nothing. What I flinch from is being confronted by some guilty person, pouring his rotten excuses down my neck."

Piron poured her a small brandy. "One often does not know the significance of what one knows. A man was killed once because he overheard but did not understand something in a railway train. This is not to alarm you."

"It does not," she said. "But your surreptitious leering . . ."

"I did not know it showed."

"You will have noted that I am on the hefty side, and at the Expensive School we were given instruction as to how to protect ourselves on all occasions. Not that most of us wanted to."

Piron picked up the brass fire irons around the dead fire. "I fight back, too."

She laughed. "Now I'm being a traitor, I think that Jay knew some strange people, but murderers . . ."

"What about Mr Jack Prat?"

"Met him twice. Oh, my dear, he's a dish, if you can bear a bed smelling of expensive cologne, or so one imagines."

"I'd better run you home. Aged P's or your own pad?"

"Here."

"I have only one bedroom."

"If I had not opted for art, I'd have been a quantity surveyor. I knew there was one bedroom! Double bed?"

"Yes," said Piron.

"If practicable, one would like to return here each night, after one's nightly teaching duties are expired," said June Smith next morning.

"One could get a cab."

"And get emotionally involved, and with a gentleman much older."

"I think you might." Piron was seated on the bed giving a gloss to his right shoe. "Or go home to Mummy at Wimbledon or wherever the green pastures may be."

"Daddy wouldn't like dolling daughters to involve themselves with mayhem."

"What time? Make up your mind, May Hem. I'll give you a key. The deep freeze is built into the larder—food dispensary as the agent described it—and there is a small bar with grog. I'm always home—at least generally—before one a.m."

"Produce the key. I'd better bring some clothes. But the more I think of it, the less I want to go back to my flat."

"Buy things at Marks and Sparks: taxi to your art classes, relish the delights of a well educated man approaching his middle years."

"Have you a middle ear, Piron?" She nibbled his left lobe.

"My assurance policy so stipulated. Have you money?"

"Never been kept since fifteen when a boy used to buy the ice-cream. Father packed me off to school. I have an account, Father's father, as grasping and far-sighted as he, having taken me out an annuity."

"This is ridiculous."

"Give me the key and don't talk about things you imperfectly perceive."

"Christ, a school-marm." Piron took the key off the ring on the dressing-table, alighted on a piece of surgical tape, and hung it above her navel.

He said, "I'm off. If a spotty youth named Hogg should call use karate quick. He is my assistant and North London randy."

You never knew about them today, thought Piron, as he went into the parking area. She might be working with Gould on a racket. Her accent was bespoke tailored, but that meant nowt. He got a taxi to the bank.

The functionary beamed at him over his priceless desk. "Your man, Hogg—astonishing accents they have nowadays—one remembers the time it had at least to be Westminister in the Bank—anyway Hogg phoned to say you had a 'lead', as he put it, on the forgeries."

"A man named McGregor had his throat cut. That is the name on the forged note. I'd like a stat of the signature."

"Certainly." The functionary rang a bell-push. "Do you think he is our man? A very tidy solution, as we don't think he had confederates."

"He might have been the peddler, say fifty-fifty. His financial origins are obscure. I have no link so far."

"You will find us generous if you do."

Eventually Piron studied the photostat, thrice enlarged. "A dashing signature."

"You can't tell. It's not a professional signature, of the type which is merely a squiggle. Virile our expert says."

"Young?"

"We have a client who married recently at ninety-three. In the banking business, Mr Piron, we find virile is as virile can. Think of the gnomes, all capable of eighteen hours in the counting house."

Piron declined a coffee and went back to his office. His old secretary diagnosed his mood and put a shot of rum in the coffee.

"Three more divorces, Mr Pee," said Hogg at his most loathsome, "an embezzlement that I don't even have to worry you about after having looked at the Accountant who has the shakes, and an industrialist who thinks his two daughters have been got at by the chauffeur."

"Investigation stops at that point, Hogg," said Piron sternly.

"I solved it intellectually, boss. He will stake them to a week abroad with necessary cholera injections. I phoned up old Sir Omicron Pie, who kicks us back fifty per on the surgery, and when he's wielding the needle he'll . . ."

"Stop it, Mr Hogg." Piron felt guilty. And faint. A croissant in bed for breakfast hardly renewed one.

"I was only looking after the interests," whined Hogg. "The P.M. said only yesterday that the basic commodities were what Old England could make or be broken by."

"How many operatives do we need?"

"We'll nut a nice little profit on six for three days, sir. Two of the divorces are caravan parks—stethoscopes on the vehicles and then burst in. Sixty quid profit on each. Sixty kicked back from old Sir Omicron, and, my word, around Grays Inn they are rubbing their hands about the fornication. The weather's changed of a sudden and, 'ow does it go? An old man's . . ."

"Look, Hogg, be silent. Six operatives, O.K. See that Sir Omicron is squared."

"Oh, the murder, Mr Pee, is I suppose upon your mind. I do counsel you that there is no money there."

"Somebody may pay us." Piron scratched his nose. One day Mr Hogg would essay to open a rather dirty little agency of his own. He should be watched, he supposed.

"Mrs Bardel is coming in, in about fifteen minutes." Hogg liked to break unpleasant surprises.

"I thought Tim would be safe in bed."

"He is hobbling. You can't keep a man with eight kids in bed."

"For God's sake spare me this homely philosophy," groaned Piron. There was a sheaf of stuff from New York, and he attended to as much of it as he could. The C.I.A. frequently briefed the Agency to answer such questions as whether Americans were liked in Europe. Now they were harping on about the importance of the herring in basic English diet.

"Do you eat herrings, Hogg?"

"In no way, sir, neither kippered, bloatered, nor canned."

"What would happen if the English couldn't get kippers?"

"One of those reports, eh?" leered Hogg who was not supposed to know about them, but you could not in practice conceal anything from his sly little eyes. "What the Yanks don't realise—pardon the term, sir, but you are an honorary gent, so to speak—is that the English'll put up with every bleedin' thing. My mum's guts have never rilly recovered from the whale meat what they made her eat in 1946, as you'd know if you heard them rumbling away. But, Lord, if Sir Alec told us that the old whale meat was necessary in the cause of peace, we'd nosh it with a will, at least those who could not afford smoked salmon would."

Piron was trying to dress this up in Pentagon prose when Mrs Bardel arrived, and with a sigh of relief he locked it in his desk.

"Timothy said I should come personally rather than phone. He knows too much about tapping to be sure that it does not happen to us. I took a shopping bag and telephoned from a call box."

"You were not followed?"

"I met Timothy when we were both working for an Agency. I used to catch shoplifters in those days. So I know the ropes. To report: a few years ago Timothy did a good turn for a man. He was working on a case—oh, not for you people—and incidentally discovered an embezzler who had a hard-luck story which Tim fell for. The man in question is born to be bad, I'm afraid, but in a financial, non-violent way. Fake companies, buying things on credit and flogging them. He does a bit in the antique line, dubious things from Ronda, that sort of thing.

He heard that Tim had had a going-over, so he telephoned—quite a long conversation. McGregor's name naturally came up. The informant knew him: I think McGregor paid him for information. There are these sources in the trade and Tim himself is not above doing a bit of it. McGregor wanted to know about forged pound notes."

Woman had a talent for drama, thought Piron. Something to do with childbirth, perhaps, and Mrs Bardel had experienced eight of these traumatic events.

"Was that all?" he asked rather coldly.

"There are a few about, not many, that is all he had to tell, except that McGregor seemed agitated."

"You have not mentioned the fellow's name."

"It's part of my husband's stock in trade. If you had another case of pinching, as you did last year, you would be glad if Tim had his very personal contacts."

It was quite true, thought Piron—the old cliché about not what you know but who you know and not giving away contacts.

"What does Tim think?"

"He's never struck anything of the kind before. Forged one-pound notes sound improbable: the risk would be too great. Tellers and people like that who handle large sums can feel a counterfeit."

"There's a certain small market in coins," said Hogg. "They are passed late at night to gents what have taken one over the eight. You can buy 'em for thirty per cent off face value, but it's only a livin'. The trick is to have a mate hold the stuff, and take them off him one or two at a time. It's a fairly safe game unless you get ambitious and you have to keep moving. Once the all-night coffee stalls were the place if you were sharp. I saw a youngster give a five-pound note once and the owner sized him up and said, 'I'll have to give you coins' and I watched him carefully count out the snide."

"And as a citizen you came to the dupe's rescue!"

"If you'd seen the knife he was using to cut up the mortadella sausage, guv'nor, you'd have gone peacefully away."

"Your cowardice curiously helps. The counterfeit boys,

humble economists though they may be, are dangerous so it seems. I expect they studied under Professor Tout, who was very down on people who interrupted the unimpeded flow of money."

Mr Hogg's acquaintances were many and curious: a certain capacity for self preservation had heretofore prevented the blackheads along his prominent throat from being excised by a razor. His wallet of obscene photographs oiled many a delicate situation, and the Agency were generous about expenses.

Coerced by Piron, who had fished a black wig and sunglasses from the office safe, Hogg glumly escorted him to an unpleasant little public house, approached through a series of narrow streets alongside the Thames. There was a sense of history about the district, but it was sad history, a whiff of generations of dull suffering, punctuated by the occasional foredoomed riot of protest. A man named Trotters, for what reason he answered to the soubriquet Piron never knew, was a cousin of the landlord and lived there, doing what paper work there was. He was a middleman in forged coins and the plain discs used for robbing slot machines.

The landlady had opened the bar and was at their entry dusting a bowl of plastic jonquils, the establishment's one aesthetic attraction. She had taut (bone supported, Piron suspected) bosoms and the style of black dress which diminishes the figure in tapering lines towards hard, blued, muscled and bony legs: the whole structure being obviously designed to keep at proper height the bird-bright black eyes, slight moustache and tight, polished black coiffure. No other human function could be imagined, or if so only in horror.

" 'Allo, you," she said to Hogg, "still pinching bums in crowded buses?"

"Lovebird," ogled Hogg, "is Trotters in labour or available for consultation?"

"Don't know yer friend!"

"Don't know old Jack Leggatt? No, I suppose not seeing he comes from Wandsworth."

"Wodger want?"

"Four quid's worth of advice."

"I dunno." She was doubtful and Piron ordered three Scotches, a fact which brightened her up. She took a sip, straightened a glass bowl of blue hard-boiled eggs, and disappeared through a door.

Trotters appeared almost immediately. Piron thought he had seen him somewhere before, a medium-sized perambulating barrel, all muscle, with two scars on one cheek.

Piron bought him the placatory drink, and took him into what Hogg described as the nook, a horrible little alcove off the bar, with a ruined upright piano and a photograph of Queen Victoria making her one and only visit to the Derby (she got herself locked in the loo, reflected Piron gloomily, and nobody was game to interfere for some hours).

"Four nickers, sis-in-law said," Trotters stipulated in his horrible voice. Piron produced them.

"A friend of mine"—the detective used the conventional underworld approach—"was looking for some pound notes."

"Dollars is better," said Trotters. "Twenty cents the last I heard, in any currency you like. There isn't good sterling stuff around at the moment. Unless he's half pissed the mark can spot the stage-money stuff at fifty paces."

Piron shrugged. "It's got to be sterling, five thousand pound-notes. And of course the friend doesn't want the mark to pick 'em. It'll be handed over in Paris. But somebody told me there are good fake fiddlies around."

Trotters finished his whisky and started on his beer chaser. "That is not common knowledge. Where did you hear it?"

"The friend knows a bank teller."

"A teller who tells." Trotters was convulsed by his own wit, Piron thought to gain time. "Ah," Trotters wiped his eyes with a blue spotted handkerchief, "you hear these rumours. Periodically old Inspector Scott, who is forgery, sends his boys asking questions. They say there is a Clever One who turns them out so they can't be detected. I never knew anybody who handled one. You get these rumours. When I was startin' out there was this rumour about somebody making di'monds, An 'oax, of course. The pound-note business might well boil down to small batches smuggled in from Europe, though as I said it's dollars that I know of, they bein' easy to forge."

Piron believed he was telling the truth as far as it lay in him.

He said: "I—I mean my mate—heard something about one McGregor."

"Wait a minute," said Trotters, "weren't there a cove of that name done in recent?" His manner subtly changed.

"It was in the papers, but the one with the cut throat was a dealer."

"I don't know anything about no McGregor." Trotters finished his beer and looked ugly.

"Thanks very much." Piron led Hogg to the door. The bar was filling with shabby-looking men and a corpulent individual with a broken nose, obviously the publican, was helping his wife. The conversation, which appeared general, died rather coldly and suddenly and Piron was glad to be out in the street which smelled of dust and stale drains.

"Christ knows why you haven't got any scars on you," grumbled Hogg.

"You should see my backside. Two bullet wounds, scars from various horse-whippings, and a tattoo saying 'Vote for Warren G. Harding'."

"It ain't funny."

"To assuage your injured feelings, take us, on expenses, to the best Scotch steak place."

Hogg caught his arm and guided him left down an alley. "Two coves following. There's a posh steak-and-oyster place on the riverside. It's well policed and we can get a cab after."

Piron had lost his appetite, but watched Hogg consume two portions of the steak-and-oyster pudding. He had always doubted that the succulent bivalves did much for you in the sex line, possibly because of the drinking which accompanied them, but like a shrewd general preparing for the fray he had two dozen Sydney oysters at ridiculous expense, and kept to a small gin-and-tonic.

"They fly straight to the whatsits," leered Hogg. "Can I congratulate you, Mr Pee? Though I always thought the effect was from the brown bread and butter, it being 'olemeal."

"For God's sake!" Piron ordered Stilton, though what it did passed his comprehension.

"Charley!" It was the waitress. Piron always forgot that Hogg had been received into the arms of the Church, no doubt in a moment of inadvertence.

"Yes, love!"

She was fully eighteen and very plump, at an age when they often seemed fascinated by Hogg's loathsome charms. "The head barman said two yobs are making enquiries about you and your gentleman friend. He tipped the wink to the potman who had a Word with them and they went. Nasty types, he said."

"Thanks, Ruby." Hogg produced his wallet with a swagger while Piron glowered behind the dark glasses. "Here's five quid. Two for the barman, two for the potman and one for you."

"Oh, thank you, Charley, for always being the gent. My quid doesn't include my tip, does it?"

"My friend's paying and he's generous on the tipping. I'll be phoning you, love."

Afterwards Piron said, "I don't know how to justify all this, what with Bardel, you . . ."

"And oysters for the lady," finished Hogg, who had acquired the most expensive liqueur on the menu. "But if you get a counterfeiter, guv, you write your own effing cheque. They strew money at your feet and give the poor sod trying to earn a penny forty years with a nice little sermon from the judge about how sacred human property is."

"I'd rather have a sermon from a judge than from you. Get your fat friend to procure a cab." He wished he had not had the Stilton.

III

IN THE EVENT the oysters were not much help. In his twenties Piron had sparkled at will: now there were times when the old witty conversation deserted him and he found himself thinking. Things died, like looks, and he wished for twenty-four hours to map out new approaches. June Smith arrived at eleven and took over supper duties with surprising efficiency. There was a nightdress presently neatly spread on Piron's bed, and a lot of bottles in the bathroom. It would get worse: already his built-in wardrobe looked crowded. She criticised the kitchen. Why did he keep his herbs in old Fruit Salt bottles? Why was there no real saffron?

She had a painting which Piron inadvisedly thought was hers, but turned out to be the fruition of a project to rehabilitate imbecile children. And something—the oysters—had given Piron a slight dose of the trots. There was a visitation at the pyjama-clad hour of one from the old maniac who had the flat next door enquiring about a rat which he said had devoured his wife's fur coat. Eventually they slept.

For him, an early riser, Piron slept late, awakening to an odour of kedgeree, a dish he particularly hated. He put on a gown and slopped into the kitchen. June looked charming. "Piron," she said, without turning from the stove, "we must rent another flat. This is far too small, particularly if we do any entertaining."

She was beautiful, gay—and managerial. Piron ate the kedgeree with a fixed smile. If you refused it, they took it as a personal insult, if you enthused they fed it every day—a Spanish girl had regaled him with a horrible egg, rice, mayonnaise and milk soup for a solid month. He tried to keep it non-committal. Piron thought that the odds were that she was a ghastly cook.

"Do you like pasta?" she asked as she helped herself, "I've got a fab collection of recipes."

"I love pasta," lied the red-headed man as his guts sent up a dismal pang.

"If you could get home early there's one with chicken liver I could make before going off to school."

"I'll be home at five thirty prompt, on feet or in a coffin." He thought that his doctor could prescribe something beforehand.

"Is your job dangerous, Piron?"

"Occasionally it could be—as when you get a psychopath or a kid in sheer panic. Most times it's humdrum: you see the windows sliding past and thank God you haven't hit the sidewalk yet."

"I'm giving my apartment up, probably the job. I can get work in London, but it means a month's notice. Old Snegg and Joyningstowe are creepy avuncular, and the associations of the place have crept up, plus the smell of violence."

"Primarily," said Piron, "the streets of that awful commuter-paradise are thick with your old bed-mates."

"Primarily, Piron, you have that kind of old-fashioned-brutal charm which one associates with nineteen-thirty film actors as presented on the TV. And you are not kidding me about that kedgeree. Why the devil did you not tell me you disliked it?"

Piron wiped his forehead. "How did you know?" He pushed the plate back.

"I may not shake the world as a painter, but I can read expressions."

"I'm a kipper man."

"I abominate the stink."

"Smoked fish, very plainly done?"

"I think, Piron, we shall settle for ham and eggs, grilled kidneys and rhubarb. By the way, I have not enquired into your financial capacities."

He told her. "Plus," he said, "some slight fiscal fiddles."

"A bit less than my dad pays his store managers."

"Could we not ponce on your father? He surely makes you an allowance."

"Nobody can ponce on my dad: he is penny intacta and always has been. A just old beast. Mother is plain silly—he picks her clothes from his yearly sales. I am the only child and told him what to do with his money when I was twenty-one and came into two thousand pounds from Great-Aunt Effie. He's offered me jobs designing bikinis—that's the kind of man he is. A chain of Swim-suit Bars, so that my art training won't be wasted."

"Freud Superstar! I wish he had not been invented."

"I've never met a man like him. He looks like you, sans the horrible accent, but you are both ruthless, I think."

"Hence a series of ruthless boy friends!"

"Hit me!"

"You'd cry copper."

"I would, in fact, hit you over the head with the steam iron which you have not wiped clean for several years."

Piron poured himself more coffee.

"So let's understand each other, Piron," said June Smith. "I can live with you."

"Would your father be irate?"

"He will probably like you. Bawl at him and swear! He's got no education except from watching the cheaper TV shows. He hates music and only reads the stuff his advertising managers bring him. That's why he's worth four million."

"What about the antiques?"

"The turn-over does not appeal to my father. I braced him for money six months ago and he immediately thought up the swim-suit caper. I'll teach for a year and save the money to start a hole-in-the-corner. I'll live rent free"—she grinned—"and I assure you Piron in five years I'll wipe Daddy's eye. He wants a life peerage, with no qualifications except the rag trade know-how, and if I've got the most famous antique business he'll come fawning round hoping to meet the fashionables. His table is so vile nobody will dine with him, nothing but steak and salmon."

He must meet Mr Smith, thought Piron.

"June," he said, "I want an excuse to hang around Frippingham. Give me your key and I'll pack your things, or come with you and do the carrying."

"We'll go this morning if you care to."

"In an hour," said Piron, and went to the bathroom.

On the pretext of topping up the oil of the car, Piron went down and used the janitor's telephone. To his secretary he dictated certain instructions to be relayed to Mr Hogg, to whom he did not feel up to talking in person.

They got to Frippingham at eleven. It wore the odd look of the sub-town where all the men, and many of the women, commuted to London by the seven forty-five, leaving behind the jovial leeches who lived off them. No slums, no poverty, merely the pleasant whiff of success.

"It's nice while it lasts," said Piron as he pulled into a parking area.

"No rumble of tumbrils at Frippingham. Just now the ladies who do not edit magazines or run model agencies are getting in the second or third family car en route for the supermarket."

"Then why did you settle here?"

"The job was here, and I liked McGregor. And to put it frankly my upbringing, however much I rebel against it, does not suit me for an ambience—as my friends say—of dark satanic mills. In the southern stockbroker belt is me, but I'm fed up with it so it's London and you."

They walked to the shop and she produced a key to the side entrance. The balustrade looked dusty and June noticed it. "That spiteful old char! Trust her to skimp her work now Julius has gone."

"Not a nice character?"

"A vicious old tale-bearer. Always talking about the tenants to Julius."

"About what?"

"What the hell does truth matter to a tale-bearer in ordinary?"

The apartment smelled of perfume. Personal possessions were not large. Three suitcases were filled with clothes and there were the books, sorted into a pile for professional removers, plus cassettes and an elaborate playing system.

"You travel light," said Piron.

"I learned that young. The father is riveted in Wimbledon. He bought a Gentleman's Library, unperused, a life subscription to Hansard, two men servants, four maids, a cook, a gardener and a bloody great ploughing machine for the garden which is never used. There is a house in Bermuda, from which he politically recoils fearing Communism, and a place in Spain whence he fears income tax. He is anchored to Wimbledon. I'm not anchored anywhere, Piron, and don't you forget it."

It was the usual stuff, thought Piron as he stacked the books, though sound enough. A middle-class intellectual perhaps, but these days they did tend to hi-jack. There was a tap at the door. June answered Mr Snegg's cautious knock.

"I thought I heard you come in," said Snegg. "Ah, it's Mr Piron." Piron thought there might be a knowing smirk around Snegg's chops.

"I'm going," said June. "I'm paid two months ahead."

"Oh, dear," said Snegg. "I was hoping you would give me a hand in the shop until it's sold—it would be good experience."

"There's a pall over the place, Sneggles. I'll come down for a coffee once in a while. In any case it won't be the same without Julius. I'll take most of the personal stuff and arrange for removers for the rest. And we might drink the last of the sherry from the glasses Julius gave me for my birthday. He gave me the sherry, too. There are some cheese biscuits in the sideboard, Piron."

McGregor's taste in sherry had been excellent, but the biscuits were on the stalish side and Piron said so.

"Gould gave them to me last week. A bit stale, like himself. He used to have a source of out-of-date groceries, slightly blown cans and suchlike. Once he tried to get me to cook an old fresh salmon that he'd bought at a British Railways disposal sale. If you don't mind coping, Sneggles, I'll pin the new telephone number on a card. What shall it be? 'Have removed. Mr Snegg, flat three, will oblige. Or phone this new number.' "

She found a tack. "Can you put this on the door, Piron, else I'll forget."

Piron took it and went out the front door. The letter 'm' is a confirmatory letter in the jargon of the trade. There it was, identical to the signature 'McGregor' on the photostat of the forged pound note. A malformed 'e' clinched [illegible] You always felt such a cad, thought Piron, as he went back to the flat and finished the sherry. Snegg seemed vaguely embarrassed. A gang? Hardly, upon thirty-six pounds a week.

Eventually they lumped three suitcases back to the car and lunched at the pub. "I'll leave you here," said Piron, "as you probably have to see friends. I've got work to do, but here is a key to the flat."

"I'd better tell Gould that we are through."

"Need you?"

"I like to tidy up. He's got a small studio here, all cigarette butts, a stink of pot and grubby sweaters."

Hogg, who in his own phrase 'wasted an evening' on a certain young lady, to the extent of three pounds which included a dubious wine, was in a foul mood when he garnered Piron's instructions. Spitefully he chose the most expensive way to Wimbledon. Smith! The directory was lousy with the name of Smith, plain or hyphened. Hogg's grubby notebook, among its lists of discreet hotels, reliable abortionists, purveyors of filthy books, listed a friendly moneylender and this slightly furtive old gentleman he consulted.

"Why, 'Ogg," said the old gentleman, "there hasn't been much new work we want info about. Trade is slow, and what we've got is reliable and steady."

"Is there a wealthy man named Smith with a tarty daughter named June?"

"Mr 'Ogg," said the moneylender, "the Smiths shall inherit

the Kingdom of the Earth, as the Good Book says, because there are so bleedin' many of them."

"He's got it now," said Hogg.

"That Smith!" the old gentleman sucked in his teeth. "I did hear his daughter had become an artist and refused to marry the chief accountant. It is 'ard if you have money and an only daughter. I told mine that she faced a life of 'oring, when I cut her off wivout a penny, or a snug existence with a chartered gentleman I picked out. She is supremely happy with six income-tax deductions and a 'oliday villa in Torremolinos. The Smith you mention is a man I know a bit about. Sometimes my son-in-law does a bit of business for him. A gentleman, and a smart business man as would cut your froat for one 'alf of one per cent. I'll give you the address if you'll tell me what it's about."

"A murder. His daughter lived in the building where it happened."

"I never advance to an artist or a journalist! That's one of the first things you learn. I knew she'd get into trouble. Dear, oh dear, are you 'elping 'er?"

"The Agency is on her side."

"I'll write you a bit of a note. Still, I suppose he'll leave the money to a foundation towards the end, like teaching Indian brats to play Beethoven. Thank God my grand-nippers are all at Cambridge."

"Not Oxford?"

"It's contaminated by all the politicians. The Chartered told me that Cambridge or Leeds was safe, but the last-named is so low!" The moneylender hesitated, then said, "I suppose you couldn't do wiv a little bit, say up to three hundred, on note of hand alone?"

"I only rob my father," said Hogg and left him cackling.

The Smiths lived in a big old mansion once owned by a Victorian dramatist. Hogg experienced some difficulty, the rich very wisely preferring to have nothing to do with sharp-looking young men with acne. He encountered a kind of butler and asserted that he had a private communication to deliver.

"The Vicar's here, partaking of the eleven o'clock drop," said the servitor. "He's paid to do the Communion if asked."

"A letter, a private letter."

"Ah, I don't know nothing of that. We do not take private letters."

It was gin, diagnosed Hogg from the smell.

"You will have to come in and wait. I will consult with Mrs Smith."

There was a chair in the anteroom, into which Mrs Smith presently surged. She was a pleasant auburn-headed lady, full of good works and perhaps a glass of sherry.

She sat her enormous behind on a small chair. "If that's Mum of the tart the guv'nor's got," ruminated Hogg, "she'll grow until she overlays him. Like mother, like daughter." Hogg always took a long look at the old lady first. In North London it was common for them to try to conceal their fat mums, but Hogg used to go round in daytime enquiring about the gas supply.

"Oh, dear, it's about our June," said Mrs Smith. "Honeyjoy, my hubby, said there had been a murder at her lodging. Every advantage she had, six pounds a week for ponies, nothing spared, as Honeyjoy says, then we found she had painted a nude. Oh, dear! The Vicar says she should be given her head."

"Was it the Vicar in the nude?" Hogg was at his unpleasantest.

"He's a thin man," said Mrs Smith pragmatically, "and who she painted was plump with side burns. But Father came to the Parting of the Ways."

"I suppose it's the same young lady," said Hogg, professionally ogling her immense charms though he preferred them on the skinny side.

"I can give you a snap." Mrs Smith rummaged. "At eighteen, playing tennis, just a few days before my hubby discovered the nude in the back of her wardrobe."

Hogg looked at the snap and wetted some blackheads. "Well developed for her age?" he suggested slyly.

"She was always a forward girl," said Mrs Smith. "It runs in the family. I was seventeen when we married and June appeared nine months to the day. I remember it was half past one in the morning."

Oh, God, thought Hogg: another three hundred nicker and he'd start an agency of his own specialising in debt collection and divorce and let that crazy old Piron stew in his own juice.

"I fear she may be in bad company," he said.

"They are all bad company these days," said Mrs Smith, "though the Vicar says there's a lot of good in them, like—oh, I forgot the name but she killed a policeman, it gets very puzzling."

"Mrs Smith," said Hogg, feeling lost, "we want to help June out of a potentially difficult situation."

"If she is in the family way," said Mrs Smith, "my hubby has heavily invested in three clinics."

"Not that, Mrs Smith, not the family but the company. Crooks. Had she any tendency to pinch things?"

"My husband keeps everything under lock and key," said Mrs Smith. "She used to rob my purse, as children do, but get at her Daddy's valuables she could not. He's so careful that he locks his teeth in a metal cabinet in the bathroom."

"She has to live," said Hogg.

"She came into some money that my hubby could not control and set herself up in art school. Mr Smith is tolerant—he employs them to design his tasteful lingerie, etcetera, and as long as they know their place he treats them well—but no, undressed nudes is what she wanted, in oils."

"Does she come to see you much?"

"Sometimes she calls to see me when my hubby is inspecting his stores. He won't set his eye on her, he only having one, until she mends her ways. Having made her bed, he says she can lie on it, though as a girl there were always servants to do it."

Hogg, hardened though he was, made his adieu and later almost welcomed Piron's presence.

"This the bint, boss?" He produced the print.

"The same," said Piron.

"Mum's got a face like a crushed bus and bozooms that knock doors in. This combines with a bird-like brain. I worked out that the girl is no better than she should be."

"She sleeps around."

"That's plain monotonous: they are all at it, subsidised by the mattress manufacturers. I meant money. I got the impression that she was not too honest. Daddy locks up his choppers of a night."

"I wonder what Daddy looks like?"

"All Daddies look like what he probably does," said Hogg with resignation, "especially those with no teeth, which makes them vicious."

"No doubt that he is rich?"

"A moneylender said he was as rich as Kruschens."

"You know, Hogg, you get these young people who like crime for kicks. Suppose old McGregor started this forgery caper and then, perhaps when his eyes went on the detail work, engaged June Smith?"

"The girls do funny things," said Hogg. "Only last week I heard of one on a charter flight to Rome who attempted to goose a respectable clergyman in mid air, and he wearing a surplice and dog-collar. Nothing is safe, Mr Pee. I 'ave to perpetually struggle for my virtue in Camden Town."

"I do wish you would be quiet, Hogg."

"That's what they say, the hussies. I have an uncle, innocently travelling to Southend, a handsome old gentleman on a pension, who had his trousers removed and was thrust off, amid lewd giggles, at a siding."

"I have never been chucked off by ladies," said Piron. "A strong generation is on the wing, no doubt."

On this, her evening off, Piron took June to an early opening, very chi-chi Indonesian restaurant specialising in things on spits. He did not mince words. "How ugly is Daddy?" he asked over the steak with peanut butter.

"He works hard. You are extraordinary, Piron! He has done nothing but work. His teeth fell out and he's got a hearing aid, but he makes eight times your salary plus expenses. So let us just eat."

"I hate the psyche bits, but it has to be asked. Do you hate the dear old pater enough to rile him by entering a life of crime?"

"Good novelist thinking. Valid? I don't know. I would not think that Father could have accumulated his wealth by sheer honesty, if you can define the term. I suppose he did his share of shuffling, but he's pleasant enough and puts up with my mother who is a girl's worst long-term reference. He has three mature mistresses and a young member of the typing pool who sits on his lap at office parties."

"If you were my daughter . . ."

"Oh, God, not putting across knees, not with *nasi goreng*."

"I'm talking of forged one-pound notes! There is one with your writing on it, one of a long trail of forged notes."

"Piron we must not kid each other!"

Piron chewed, then said: "I play for keeps, June. I spotted it when you wrote the note to put on the door. And the note has the superscription 'McGregor'."

"You are serious. I can smell it over the spices, but so wrong," she chuckled. "Fix me for fornication, addle me for adultery, but forgery is not in the lexicon."

"I thought of McGregor, dear."

"Much money? The Father always says simply concentrate on the money corner."

"Three thousand a year, say, without tax."

"From my Agatha Christies it's fourteen years in quad when they catch you."

"On the scale it's done it is not a large-scale operation."

"One wishes you did not talk like my father."

"No kidding, June!"

"I'm serious enough, Piron, and I do not see McGregor forging notes. He seemed honest between the limits of dealing."

"The fact is that his name is written on a forged note."

"I'm an absent-minded person, Piron. Sometimes, in the shop, somebody would leave money. I am quite capable of getting it mixed up with my own. I usually scribbled his name on an envelope. There is the possibility I wrote his name on a note. For the life of me I can't remember doing it."

"I suppose they looked at McGregor's own quarters, but you might use a room in a cheap office block. Would he have had the knowledge? I'm assuming McGregor somehow gave you the note."

"Counterfeiting was not in the course, but I do know the usual stuff about photographic reproduction. McGregor was a practical man and he could use a camera, though today they are pretty foolproof. Had he given his mind to it, he could probably have forged notes. I dare say you could find out how to do it or work it out yourself. What would seem to cancel out such a possibility is the problem of passing the stuff. How is it done?"

"For six pounds a day," said Piron, "you eat, buy cheese, go occasionally to a race meeting and try to back a nonstarter, or if not the favourite in certain races, have a meal in a strange restaurant, move about, and it might take a year for the forgeries to be picked up. You do not pass more than two pounds at a time because of the numbering of the notes, which you cannot vary."

"That again, I cannot see. Julius knew nothing of horse racing and had barely heard of the Derby: he was very conservative about his choice of restaurants and never went to more than half a dozen. The same with hotels. When on a day's travelling he used mostly to carry a couple of sandwiches in his briefcase."

"He must have cooked at home, I suppose."

"He did not eat much. When he did it was grilled meat and a frozen vegetable. Always the finest meat. He had a very expensive and fancy electric griller. He used to say that in the part of the world he came from there was a shortage of grilling meat and as a boy he vowed if ever he could, he would eat little else. He seemed to thrive on it."

"A strange man!"

"I do not think so, against his early environment. How the devil would we have even survived? He clung to dealing, because it was the only fixed point in his life. I asked him once what he would do when he retired, and he answered 'Die!'"

"And yet he had curiosity which made him pry."

"I'm afraid that is fair enough."

"Did he ever mention Jack Prat?"

"Gould knew him and told me he was one of the high-powered international money men—a tall, handsome gnome. I got the impression that Jay hoped he could get a job with him. I only saw him at the exhibition: I did not like him much. Julius did ask me once and I said I'd only heard of him."

By this time they had finished and Piron went to the phone.

"Jerry," he asked his informant, "where is one Jack Prat likely to be?"

"Why should you be messing with Jack Prat?"

"I love him. I want to take him to my bosom."

"Harrods do a nice line in vipers, Piron, but you know best. I'll give you the address. It's a private club, and you might or might not get in. Bridge and poker, no ostentation but you could lose three hundred over the night. Free snacks, the usual kindness, no rough stuff but keep the voice down and the cheque negotiable . . ."

"Do you play poker?" asked Piron as he settled the bill.

"No, only black-jack and bridge."

"A club where Mr Prat waits for victims. No cheating, just Prat and expertise!"

"I'm good at black-jack. Daddy couldn't play the usual children's games, so he taught me the odds."

"Better make it early, and be charming to Mr Prat."

They walked through the sleepy evening, savouring warmth from the day's concrete. It was perhaps an hour, hand in hand. The club looked rather like a small, modest hotel: there was a commissionaire in regalia; a little ante-room with a polite young man at a desk.

"Mr Piron and Miss June Smith to see Mr Prat. We are not members."

"I don't know, I'm sure." His shrewd little eyes priced Piron's suit, lingered momentarily on June's ruby bracelet. "I'll have to ask him." He got up and vanished through a swing door.

Prat, tuxedoed, apparently recently shaved, accompanied him on his return. Bland and benevolent he greeted them. "I did not know you were addicts."

"I play bridge," said June. "My father is mindless except for cards."

"Poker for me," said Piron. "Hours in smoke-filled hotel rooms with the guns parked in the wash basin spent playing it."

"No guns here," smiled Prat, but Piron sensed he was disconcerted a little. "Come with me. There is one poker table going, and we are waiting for a fourth for bridge."

They entered a discreet little bar. Piron ordered Campari and June a single whisky. Prat, who paid, drank what Piron thought was water coloured to look like whisky. "I thought you would be crowded," said Piron.

"Except for tournaments, the action is in the afternoon, ceasing around six thirty—the dowagers mostly: then it is quiet until about ten when the clubmen types come in for a rubber or two."

"Well, we might as well pass an hour, if you could accommodate us, Mr Prat. Bridge for Miss Smith, poker for this bluff old American sucker."

The main card-room was largish, furnished in impeccable taste. Not for the first time Piron wondered why you spent so much time in such nice surroundings with a deck of cards. Prat walked ahead: Piron took the opportunity of asking June whether she really could play bridge.

"Daddy works percentages, Piron. As a little girl he taught me bridge."

The three people at the bridge table looked bored, wealthy and decent and Piron left her in their company. The poker set were sharper, Canadians looking for a little action. The game, nevertheless, was orthodox enough. In an hour he lost twelve pounds, but mainly because of the way the cards fell. At the end of that time the bridge tables began filling and a minority favoured poker, which gave Piron the opportunity to contribute his share towards the house cover charge and bow out. A snug little racket, he thought: if you had two or three of them it added up into a pretty good investment, though running costs would be high. He could not see June, but found her in the half-filled bar.

"I broke about even," she said, "thanks mainly to my partner who is damned good. You would not want to be a beginner here. I always wonder where the gambling money comes from."

"Fairy gold."

"The fairies must own a Mint."

"I just wanted to see Prat in his environment, but it's all clean and hygienic . . . hallo."

Prat came through the swing door from the foyer. With him was the dapper gangster known as the Dickybird, dressed nicely in a man-about-town outfit. His glance caught Piron a little too late, for the big red-head had left his bar-seat and was right before him.

"Remember me, Dicky? Do you want some curry?"

The Dickybird, incongruously whispering in the cause of respectability, said something vile.

"Now, Piron," eased Prat, "all gentlemen together. We have our methods for non-gentlemen."

"I thought he was your boy, Prat! Now I know!" He stamped on the Dickybird's foot.

"Now! No trouble here," snapped Prat, grabbing the Dickybird's right wrist as it snaked up to his lapel.

"You're a punk who can't make trouble for my little sister who is only nine!" said Piron.

"Get out!" said Prat, sweating.

"When I finish my drink. And Prat—I'm not McGregor!"

"I don't like that!"

"You are not supposed to," Piron assured Prat.

He walked back to June and finished his drink. "Big trouble," she asked, "and who is the tough man?"

"Yclept the Dickybird, and not tough under bright lights, but we should leave before he turns them off."

She fussed with a lipstick. Piron turned his head. Both the Dickybird and Jack Prat were nursing a drink. Their eyes were downcast, and for the first time Prat looked evil. "Get going," he said.

The street outside was well lighted and there was a cab depositing a couple at the club. Piron was thankful to take it.

June after all provided him with kippers for breakfast and he wondered uneasily if she contemplated matrimony. He brushed his teeth, kissed her and drove the office car to Tim Bardel's. Mrs Bardel, embarrassed as house-proud women are, scurried to remove the cleaning utensils and place a bright new coverlet on the bed on which Bardel reposed, as if she expected Piron to believe the brightly burnished interior happened by supernatural agency.

"Just to report progress, Tim," said Piron and covered the salient points.

"I have not been idle, Piron," Bardel motioned towards the telephone by his bedside. "As you know I've got a lot of contacts."

Piron nodded.

"Some of the people around McGregor were a little on the ropey side. Snegg, for instance, is a quiet little gentleman, but was co-re four times which cost him his savings and a chance of a headship." Bardel looked as pious as a man with eight legitimate issue can. "Still waters run deep!" he added sententiously.

"He doesn't sound precisely *still*," commented Piron.

"Miss June Smith, the daughter of a retail-store millionaire, gathers up boy friends and works for a living." Bardel sounded scandalised, for whatever reason.

"At present she shacks with me."

There was a slight rattling sound from Mrs Bardel, within earshot trying surreptitiously to remove a bucket of soapy water concealed behind the Victorian sideboard with its plethora of hideous little shelves.

"Believe me, Piron, the marriage bed is best, and I should know, by Christ!" It was the Tim Bardel version of unctuousness.

"For the present purposes Miss Smith is covered. I might have suspected her, but with Daddy's dough and Mummy a nit, we might think of her as out of court."

"She sounds fond of courting." Bardel became as risqué as he ever did, a life of peering at copulating couples through transom windows having dulled his taste for porn. "However there's a funny thing about Captain Joyningstowe, late of the cartographical department of the War Office. I thought he was part owner of this old-fashioned but large bookshop—Joyningstowe, Gardner and Hampton."

"Isn't he?"

"Since 1930 it's been owned by a family named Green who bought it lock, stock and barrel in bankrupt condition. I got a friend to see young Green—the old man died—and he says they nursed it back into quite a nice business. Joyningstowe is the only link with the past. He specialises in eighteenth-century diaries, etcetera. If something in that line comes they phone him, or in any case he often comes in for half an hour to browse around. They commission him occasionally to attend sales, and at Christmas time he acts as a salesman on Saturdays. A courteous, old-worlde olde cocke, forsooth. But in a good year he might get three hundred pounds from Green and some Yuletide Sherbet—he is a conoozer of fine Scotch. Pension commuted years ago, declares Green, who thinks he must have some other source of income. Is he your Mr Six by Six? Suppose Julius spotted it? As a lineal descendent of the poor blokes driven from the Temple, the thought of tampering with the currency would be anathema."

"A lot of conjecture," said Piron, "but thanks. I should have checked on Snegg and Joyningstowe."

"Preoccupied with other checking," snorted Mrs Bardel, and did not say goodbye.

He caught June talking to his thrice-weekly cleaner, a salty old lady who gave the red-headed man the famous Cockney leer. However June seemed to get on well with her, and Piron interrupted a spirited description from Mrs Cockshutt, which transpired to be the cleaner's name, though Piron had not heard it before, as to how she disciplined Cockshutt if he got pissed on bingo nights.

Waiting until this formidable female had at last taken the vacuum cleaner from its lair, Piron decided that he had better not take June into the bedroom, and settled on the kitchen, cleaned by June and rather pointedly deodorised.

"I have only once, and as a small girl, been seduced in a refrigerator, Piron."

"It always gives me sciatica, but please, love, what do you know about Joyningstowe?"

"The gallant Capting? Ex Army, dabbled in water colours, lives off the family bookshop. Parasitical, as Jay Gould called him, who would be done away with at the first touch of Red Rev."

"Bardel, who is generally accurate, says he has not much visible means of support. The family business was sold as far back as 1930. He had some part-time work there—three hundred pounds a year—but he had amortised his pension. He lived quite well."

"Oh, God," she said. "I mean he's *decent*, not cruel."

"That note with 'McGregor' written on it in your writing?"

"I could not stand witness against him."

"It's a game, love, and you have to play by the rules. If you are honest that's how you play. If you are crooked, well there are the other rules."

"There was a time, a year ago, when I was in the shop alone," she said in a low voice. "Joyningstowe used to pay his rent, month in advance, in cash. An eccentricity, but an old man, after two world wars, should be allowed it, including his habit of being sloshed on Scotch in holiday time. He came in, and fumbled with his wallet, giving me pound notes. He went out, trying to keep his back straight. I remember that I'd drawn out fifty pounds the previous day, the last of my aunt's legacy, to buy equipment for my hi-fi. There was no envelope about—Julius kept his stationery upstairs. I scribbled 'McGregor' on the top note and stuck the wad in my purse. I guess—but cannot remember—that I handed it to Julius when he came back."

"I'll have to pass this upstairs, June."

"I think I'll pass you going down."

"In any case we can smile wryly."

The man Piron saw at Scotland Yard was elderly and wise. He said: "Frankly this has been a bugbear to me, constant bullets flying over the inter-com."

"The Agency wants no credit. The Bank will pay a handsome fee. There's no question of smart Americans being about." Piron is quick to get a point.

"Would the girl's evidence stand up?"

"Her father is a millionaire and juries accept that as proof of rectitude."

"We'll search this man's flat, a general search warrant covering the building on account of McGregor's death. It's unusual, but in view of the fact that there is a slight doubt about the weapon we should be able to get it. Your interest, I take it, is the assumption that Joyningstowe murdered McGregor?"

"It is at least a smear large enough to get my client, Bardel, off the hook. And as a quid pro quo, would you phone me within reasonable time?"

They shook hands.

This was rather more than Piron did on his return to his office, where Hogg was loquacious. "Your young lady, guv'nor. I took the liberty of watching you leave your abode, thinking you might want a check. The young lady, elegantly clad, went down in the lift at nine fifty and into the public call box fifty yards away. I sidled up, looking for a lost wallet, while she was dialling the number, but she was abusive. Obscene language she used while threatening to call the police. Very suggestive, seeing you have a phone which she is presumably"—Hogg smirked—"entitled to twiddle."

Wearily, Piron dialled his flat. The cleaner said that the young lady, 'ever so nice', had been gone for forty minutes.

Piron managed to find an errand for Hogg, and settled back to a bout of kippery indigestion and the *Daily Telegraph.* At mid-day the phone rang with his friend from Scotland Yard on the line. "It was so, Piron," he said. "A back room, with impedimenta, and five hundred made notes. It had two first-class locks. Joyningstowe is out: I have men waiting for him. He has not been sighted at the shop, or his club."

"A mistake, I suppose," said Piron. "A trifle drunk one day and puts a forgery with his rent to McGregor who spots it."

"Hang on," said the Scotland Yard man, "something is coming through. I'll let you listen in."

Peter Joyningstowe had died like a gentleman, aged seventy-three, upon a bench in Green Park, quickly from cyanide, his head, perhaps ironically, plunged into the *Church Times.* A notebook contained a valedictory: "I thought that I was entitled to a small but adequate income. I have harmed no one. The banking system is a leech upon the human race and I merely deprived them of a small drop of blood. Having no living relatives I have scrawled a Will leaving what I have to Samuel Snegg, not that I like him, but that, as myself, he is a poor devil. I have no knowledge of McGregor's murder. I operated alone and had no accomplices."

Piron lunched dolefully alone off soup and an omelette. The Captain had been tipped off it was all too clear by whom.

Eventually, when he could put it off no longer he drove to Frippingham, and after a little trouble found the gaunt technical college, an Edwardian remnant chiefly distinguished by its two straggling outside lavatory blocks and an air of acute depression. Great art it might produce—though Piron had never heard of any—but it seemed to him eminently suitable for teaching engraving upon tombstones. However he was cheered by the sight of the young woman behind the switchboard cum reception desk. He thought she might double as model for the life classes. Sideways in her swivel chair she was eating toffees. At Piron's throat-clearing she swung round, her splendid bosom dislodging a telephone directory.

"Yiss?" She had one of the regional accents that Piron never could place.

"I want to see Miss June Smith."

"I fink she's in. Rum twenny-three up the 'all." She gestured with a toffee and Piron swiftly nipped it from her fingers, leaving her, cheeks swollen with partly masticated goodies, goggling at him. Strictly a figure woman figured Piron, going through dirty swing doors.

June Smith had her own cubby-hole and was apparently marking home-work. Piron entered without knocking, and straddled the kitchen chair reserved for students.

"Joyningstowe suicided in Green Park. He had a locked room in his flat with forging equipment, but left a note denying anything to do with McGregor's murder. You must have tipped him off and caused him to do it."

Her eyes filled with tears. "Damn you," she said, "you love hounding people."

"I told you this morning, it's one side of the fence or the other. Straddle it and you get splinters."

"I'll collect my things and get out."

"Better do it civilised. I'll sleep in the living-room. You can call a cab and get the hell out of my hair."

She threw a book at him, slightly cutting his face. In the lobby the receptionist was still eating toffees.

Inspector Feld was in and greeted Piron with forced bonhomie. "Well, you made me look a prize fool."

"Not so," said Piron, "I just got a break."

"I don't think I was to blame for not searching those apartments. It's not procedure and I doubt whether I could have got a warrant. Top Yard brass is another matter."

"Seems strange nobody should have spotted the locked room over the years."

"Before conversion it was a kind of stockroom for grain—the building was the old grain merchant's. No windows and a narrow door: it looks like the entrance to a closet. The architect didn't know what to do with it. He tells me that the best he could think of was a dark room or something of that nature. Joyningstowe had McGregor's char in twice a week, but she's the kind of woman who does the minimum. Still, it must put your man, Bardel, in the clear. No doubt the old Captain slipped down the back stairs, picked up the knife and did him in." He sighed. "The Coroner won't be pleased at having to bring in a 'persons unknown' verdict."

"There's a faint flaw in the case. If McGregor had told Joyningstowe that he wanted to see him, you would have thought it would be in one of the two apartments."

Feld fiddled with a pencil. "I thought of that, but it could well be that Joyningstowe knew that McGregor was on to him, was familiar with his habits, and came down the back stairs when he heard McGregor slip-slop down."

Piron said: "I make this clear because it is the Agency's policy to co-operate with the law enforcement agencies, as my countrymen so quaintly call them, even to the C.I.A. I find Joyningstowe's guilt doubtful."

"It was not the C.I.A. that got old Miss Traylor drunk on

the day of the inquest! Oh, muggins me had enough I.Q. to fathom that one out! I do not trust you, Piron,—how does it go?—'a horny hand and strong breath'."

"Always a privilege to meet Elizabethan scholars. I'll use cold cream and chlorophyll for your benefit."

"You are stalking me, friend," the Inspector grinned. "Come to tawses."

"A certain Jay Gould! Gould looked a smart, blackmailing type on the only occasion I saw him. Were they in concert?"

"Small towns like this are not complex," said Feld. "The stuff the novelists write about—vicar's wife seducing the innocent, old Mr Smith burying still-born infants under the cabbage patch like the Welsh writers used to go on about—is mostly untrue. A little wife-swapping, tax evasion and genteel drunkenness, that's all we have, plus traffic offences. I would imagine, according to the record, that Gould is harmless enough."

"Thanks, we should have dinner one day."

"Glad to extend the general hand of forgiveness."

A nice policeman overall, thought Piron afterwards, interposed between the loathsome English middle class, preoccupied with petty fiddles, and dubious law. He had, by cunning, secured June Smith's keys to the building and to this he repaired. As he anticipated, a plainclothed man materialised down the stairs. He explained himself. "The Inspector knows I am on the case."

"He's not dumb," said the Sergeant. "He telephoned through. We cannot stop you, but it would be pleasanter if we co-operated."

"An Estab. word that works one way, but you can snoop on me as much as you care. Is Snegg in?"

"So prostrated with grief he can hardly work the till in the shop. Did you know he was Joyningstowe's beneficiary?"

"No. How much?"

"His solicitor says sixteen hundred pounds in bonds. Then there's the contents of the flat which will make a pretty penny, acceptable to such a permanently pecunious person."

"Mind the pees, old friend, or you'll be waiting in a queue."

"The boss said you were a funny man."

"Mirthful mayhem a must," leered Piron and went up the stairs.

The door of Joyningstowe's apartment was open. He walked in.

"Make yourself at home," greeted a constable, incongruously seated on the edge of an Empire chair. Piron stood back and appraised. Good furniture, on the uncomfortable side except for an old leather club chair in front of bookcases, a sketch by William Etty, and, slightly apart from the rows of paper backs, some two hundred rare books. The 'personal effects', as the jargon went, would certainly fetch a pretty penny.

"The books would be worth two thousand," said the constable, "at a bare minimum. I collect in a very modest way: these are all prime copies, many inscribed. I suppose he had opportunities to acquire the odd bargain."

"Can I see the counterfeiting room?"

"With shrill cries, the Scotland Yard blokes carried the contents down to a security van. I might tell you in confidence that it looked so simple that I wonder why I'm wearing down my arches. There's nothing to see except some fancy lighting. Only his prints around. All I can tell you is that he lived well; German wines, smoked salmon, caviar, all sorts of cans, high on the hog while he had it. Poor old bugger, if you look at it from one point of view."

Piron had been peering at a row of paintings, modern, and of the Barcelona school. "Strange how many old Army types know their painting values. An eye for the terrain, possibly."

"I dare say he believed the world owed him a living," said the constable. "We come across it all the time."

"I'll go and see Snegg," said Piron and went down by the back stairs. The retired schoolmaster was in the small office in which McGregor had been murdered. Piron noted that there was a peep-hole from which, seated at the desk, you could see into the shop. Snegg appeared to be making out bills.

"This is terrible, Mr Piron," Snegg pushed his spectacles over his eyebrows and looked down his nose.

"He was broke," said Piron, "and realised that forgery was

easy. He must have had art training. He was not greedy, just six pounds most days, but in the end the percentages catch up with you. You inherit, I understand."

"It was kind of him," said Snegg. "We had not much in common, he being of good family and I a poor dominie out of scholarship stables. He knew I had suffered constant financial reverses . . ."

"In bed," thought Piron but kept a poker-face.

"I'm not sure that I should accept the money," said Snegg, in a tone which Piron recognised. He responded to the gambit. "There is no proof that his estate had any connection with forgery, so you would be justified in accepting it."

Snegg obviously seized this straw with alacrity.

"I suppose you had no idea that he was up to anything?"

"I envied him," said Snegg, simply, "as part heir to a profitable business. Of course in your job you would often encounter hindsight. Joyningstowe always seemed to have masses of small change, one supposes from changing the counterfeit. Again, once I had to go to London on a slight matter of personal business, with a couple of hours between appointments. I caught the train with Joyningstowe. I said that it would be interesting for me to see the workings of the bookshop. He jobbed me off rather obviously. But at the time I did not think too much of it: after all I suppose there are professional secrets that one cannot divulge. In himself he was elegant, a trifle professionally so, but that may be a reaction from the difference in our origins."

The swing door leading to the stairs opened. It was Miss Traylor, bibulous as revealed by a leftward list. "Sneggle!" she began, carefully focusing. "And what do I find. An imposther who shaid he worked in my family's school! A generation of wipers."

"I taught you to ski," joked Piron.

"And I broke my leg. It's true I had had a little drink to warm me, but to phresume in the language you used to my dear Mother is quite unforgivable. I forget *your* name but *you* are Snegg." She swung round.

"Yes, Miss Traylor," said the little schoolmaster.

"They tell me the Captain's dead."

"As a doornail, poor fellow, *felo de se*," said Snegg grimly.

"I wanted to consult you." Miss Traylor brandished a voluminous handbag, and for the moment entered reality. "He used to give me money to change for him, on ten per cent commission. Such a sympathetic man. A few pounds means a lot to me in these days of cruel taxation. When I was in Switzerland it was threepence in the pound. If only Mr Barber were a Swiss, yodelling away as they do, and there are the wonderful cow bells the others could wear." She wavered and Mr Snegg deftly inserted a chair underneath her.

"How much have you got?" said Piron.

"A hundred and three pounds and forty-nine pence, a tin of York ham, thirty-six bouillon cubes, four bottles of Marmite, six double damask handkerchiefs with red spots, and a cigar. You see, I had to change them, not more than two at a time. I had no idea that the dear man made them. It must be easy. There was a girl at the School who used to forge her Daddy's cheques, but she was an American and they were always troublesome in spite of morning cold showers. I feel quite faint."

Mr Snegg pulled open a drawer and produced half a bottle of cherry brandy and a small glass. He poured and said: "Julius often believed in closing a bargain with a drop of this."

Miss Traylor sucked and goggled gratefully.

"I should keep the groceries," said Piron, "because such things only embarrass the constabulary, like the sturgeon which are properties of the Queen. Give Mr Snegg the pound notes. I will be witness, he will scribble a receipt."

Miss Traylor dived into her handbag. Piron checked the first ten notes. The numbers were the same: they had been slightly creased and dirtied.

"This is irregular," said Snegg.

"I'll countersign," Piron said.

"Perhaps a little drop for our nerves," said Miss Traylor. "I remember the evenings we enjoyed in Helvetia, as they used to say. The fish was very poor, but the cheese excellent."

IV

PIRON SPENT HIS evening, clad in pyjamas, lounging on the day bed and watching television until he turned off the light, unable to sleep.

At midnight he heard the front door open, and afterwards bathroom signals. Eventually he dozed, kicking the clothes aside.

Light blinked through the half-draped windows at six. He was dreaming of a Siamese cat he once had and which slept on his shoulder.

"Piron," said a soft voice, "I thought better the devil I know."

He was dreaming, thought Piron, but at seven thirty found that he was not.

"Stay or go away," he said at eight. The day bed was not meant for two and his spine ached.

"Stay! I was a fool. But you buy pyjamas and forsake those ghastly underpants."

"In return for kippers, no pasta, but tripe, steak-and-kidney pudding and definitely nothing you read of in the women's mags."

"To hear is to obey."

"Hell," said Piron, "the Bank is probably pestering the office. What say a quiet morning at the British Museum then a steak?"

"I have to see an employment agent and it's not Mrs Cockshutt's day on."

"I'm used to cleaning the place in thirty-five minutes."

"So the bedroom closets look, and the loo needs Harpic. You run away on your deceitful errands and, after your bloody smoked fish, I shall roll up sleeves and endeavour to take the sordid out of our shack."

It took a woman to take you down, thought Piron in the bath. He remembered that a neighbouring cat had come through the window and made away with the loo brush six months ago. He had not got round to buying another. The monstrous regiment of women, a quotation so often misapplied.

June was not a bad cook, though smoked haddock was not much of a criterion. He said so. "You seem to go in for cheapness in buying," she said, like a slowly ticking time-bomb. "The haddock is coloured cod, messed around by industrial chemists named Arthur Someone."

One thing about having a woman around, thought Piron, as he got the car out, was that it made you prompter in to work. In a way it cheered him up. He found both Hogg and his secretary boggling at the munificent offering delivered by the Bank's Special Messenger whose top-hat had overawed the tough old secretary.

"We know what eff to choose in future, Mr Pee," said Hogg. "Sixty quid for fornication and seventeen hundred, expenses to be agreed later, for forgery. Auditors pay more than adulterers, screevers more than screwers, and a good forged fiddlydid is better than a woman."

"Really Mr Hogg," said the old secretary, deftly easing Piron's agate paper-weight off the edge of the desk and on to Hogg's left foot.

When he had finished bleating with pain, Hogg, who is frightened of the secretary, contented himself with a malevolent glance and the question: "This clears Tim Bardel?"

"A dirty clearance, in that the Director would not put a case into court. I'd rather it was clean cut. There is no evidence that Joyningstowe did the killing. What impressed me is the fact he could have taken the implements out of the flat and dumped them in the river. Then he would be safe."

"Somebody watching and blackmailing him. Somebody home a lot," said Hogg. "Snegg or a certain young lady; perhaps it was McGregor, but on the other hand it could have been done indirectly, by telephone or letter, and Joyningstowe could have wrongly suspected McGregor."

"Snegg is devious," said Piron.

"If you arst me about deviations, look to the ladies," said Hogg.

"Should I take a note, Mr Piron?" asked the secretary.

Without answering Piron took his hat off the rack. He knew when the English ganged up on him.

The Agency operates in an unfashionable part of London, the comparative ease of parking offsetting the inconvenience of its nasty little streets and alleys. Other firms were getting the idea, mused Piron, his semi-slum landlord was raising the rents, and soon he thought that the Agency would have to move to even sleazier pastures. He would probably lose Hogg who considered the present environment low, but he had an eye on a certain smart youth they used for casual spying upon parked cars at night.

He collected the car and drove to the nearest taxi rank, where he had an arrangement to park while he switched over, progress being what it is. He was driven to the office of the monthly magazine which specialised in objets d'art. Once, three years ago, Piron, professionally, had caught the accountant paying himself for non-existent articles, a frequent literary device. By protesting past services, he got in to see the manager, a man compounded of bluffness, humour, alcoholism and piles, a mixture common to those who guide the progress of magazines.

"We put in a new accountancy system, Piron," said the manager. "Only I steal and that is expense accounts and journeys to Bermuda in search of copy. What brings?"

"You might want a favour one day."

"Such as a case of Scotch!"

"Can be done! I merely want to know what big sale of old silver is being bandied about."

"You're talking of hens' teeth. You can sell any choice bit of silver. There is no big deal that I know of. The Americans snap up anything from teaspoons up as a hedge. It's about the best investment there is: paint fades, maddened people attack sculpture, they artificially inflate diamonds and gold, but silver, oh, my God!"

"McGregor, who was murdered, probably was middle-man for a large collection."

"Nonsense. I'd have heard. We get part of our money doing a private service advising special subscribers about stuff likely to come on the auction block. We've got a chain of informants, house agents, auctioneers and the like. We scratch their backs, they scratch ours. I, *me*, put my hard-won savings into choice silver."

"You knew McGregor?"

"I know them all: a medium-sized operator, not much imagination, but well thought of. God knows why anybody should want to knock him off."

"When does the next issue appear?"

"Part is printed, the colour and monochrome photos: text pages go to press at three this afternoon. Subscribers' copies will go out tomorrow morning: bookstall orders in the afternoon, or so, in these times, one damned well hopes."

"I want a small displayed ad."

"It will cost you dear because we'd have to open a page."

"Money no object!"

"Oh, why cannot all advertisers be such sweet understanding boys?"

Piron reached over for a scratch pad and wrote: 'Amateur wishes to acquire collection of old silver, choice pieces only. Write or telegraph Box . . .'

"Biggish type," he said, "and if anything turns up send a boy round to my office."

"So what goes on?"

"Perhaps someone is trying to dispose of fake silver."

"The very devil!" said the manager. "A quite large number of superb artisans have been laid off due to falling demand for new stuff and some of them would naturally be open for work on reproduction ware. The boss would do the ageing if he knew anything about simple metallurgy. Are you acting for the Police?"

"Only indirectly," said Piron.

In fact half an hour later he did report to the wise old man at Scotland Yard.

"I doubt," said his friend, "that any very large collection of silver of British origin could be peddled without the trade press knowing of it. That leaves the other countries. I'll get on to Customs."

Those professional grinders averred that no great quantity of old silver had entered the country over the past three years.

"That's that," said Piron's informant, "and I was going through Interpol files the other day and there has been no great theft of such ware."

"Leaving forgery."

"We occasionally get a case of passing-off. However silver buyers are registered, and we would have heard if there was any upsurge in the sale of metal. And manufacturers of silver articles are all known. I don't think we can intervene—too many influential people to get questions asked in the House. I'll get you typewritten lists while we go and have a beer. Then I'll give you a verbal description of the one or two scoundrels: it's a clean trade generally, but as usual there are a few runts in the litter."

They spent an hour sipping lager. When they went back the Superintendent passed over a carbon copy and, putting on his reading glasses, went over the names. "This man, nicknamed Holy Joe for some reason, might be your best bet. He's a shifty creature and financially strictly peanuts, but he knows everybody in the silver trade. We've had cause to question him a couple of times. The name, Forrest, is his real one and he is a Scot, though they say he might be shot if he ever went back."

"He doesn't make money?"

"So snaky is the gentleman that he has tripped himself up all through life. You know the kind of man, unable to run straight. He has a little office in the City but is rarely in it. His wife will phone through to get him if you exude a little smell of money and, my word, how Sammy runs back." The policeman scratched his pointed chin. "On the whole I think Forrest is your man, if the man indeed exists."

Piron thanked him and went through the heavy afternoon traffic. 'Forrest. Agent', said an old brass plate. Inside there were two small desks, three Bentwood chairs, worn linoleum, a strong smell of fried fish proceeding from a piece of newspaper in a waste-paper basket, and a rather pleasant-looking woman in her fifties who was operating the oldest typewriter Piron had ever seen.

"Mrs Forrest," he said, "I've come to see your husband."

Her calm eyes appraised him.

"There could be money in it for him."

"A policeman?"

"Private investigator."

Obviously a woman of few words, she consulted an old exercise book and dialled. Piron elaborately did not listen. There appeared, however, some delay in getting Forrest. Finally she replaced the handset and said in a louder voice: "He's five minutes away by cab and you can sit down and wait."

Forrest's desk was at least dusted, clean and bare except for a trade magazine. An importunate fly bothered Piron's neck. For some reason he expected a eupeptic fat man with gold teeth but Mr Forrest was a tall, thin fellow with the faint look of a disappointed hangman. Sixtyish, well groomed except that to Piron's expert nose there was the faintest whiff of seediness about him.

Piron produced a card. "Always glad to help the authorities."

The thin man absently opened a drawer.

"No need to switch the recorder on, Mr Forrest."

Cold eyes surveyed Piron. Probably a police informer, thought the detective.

"I'm a busy man," said Forrest, but quite gently.

"I want to know the names of any craftsmen who might be tempted to forge old silver."

"You're asking me a lot, sir."

Piron shrugged. "I'll pay you a hundred, but it will have to be a cheque." There was some telepathy between Forrest and his wife. "Win, lose or draw," said Forrest, "the cheque in advance, plus one pound for the taxi."

The red-haired detective wearily took out his cheque book. Forrest looked at it with an expression of sorrow. "There's wickedness in the world, Mr Piron."

"I did not pay a hundred nicker for an exposition of Presbyterianism, and don't carry on about Mary Queen of Scots."

Piron could have sworn both Mr and Mrs Forrest were amused.

"Forby, which is the only Scots they understand, you are a man of the world. I would not want to do what the horse tipsters do, sir, in giving you half the field as possibles. There is unemployment in the industry and a man has to live: it seems to get more difficult as you get older. Mind you I do not say that anything criminal is meant. A man employed to make a reproduction piece does not *have* to make enquiries as to what end. Oh, no!"

"I'm not seeking to prosecute anybody. I just want to know on behalf of a client whether somebody has a swag of good forged silver, say in the fifty thousand class, maybe much more."

Forrest picked at the lobe of one ear. "I've been thinking. There is a character named Fat Giles, one of the best finishers in the business but addicted to drink. When the retrenchment, as they call the sack these days, came, he was the first to go. They discovered three pregnant typists and two cupboards filled with empty Scotch bottles in his wake. He would be on odd jobs, I thought, working for small jewellers when he wasn't smashed. He dropped out of the usual haunts, we're a close-knit loyal community like the Arabs. But chance to tell, I saw him the other day, at a pub in Richmond. Good suit, Bloody Marys which he loves, Scotch steak, flashy, with a tart with him, he being a rare man for the muff. I've known Giles for years, God blimey, lent him bits of money and gave him the address of my solicitor when he said he fell down on top of a lady at a party, she mistaking his action. But Giles with any money is impossible: 'e always spends what he earns and he ain't employed in the Trade!"

"And his address?"

"Another tenner."

This time Piron produced the notes.

"Ta. I can only give the address of the pub. Once a man gets the habit of going to a pub, he continues it. It's the old Earl Gray, half way up the Hill, but off to the side. A discreet sort of place with good food. Somebody told me they might rebuild and that the new company would sell off the contents. A man occasionally gets a snip out of an affair like that. Fat Giles was having his drink in the snuggery before taking his woman into the dining-room and he refused to meet my eye, so I bumped into him in the gents and said 'Hallo, Fat, my boy'. In all innocence, like. He kind of bridled, but had to say, 'Hallo, Joe'. A silly way of greeting, in Argyll we just scowl and grunt. 'What are you doing?'

says I. He replies, 'I got a job travelling in bathroom fittings'. He is a short pimply fellow with a fair beard."

"You haven't heard of any big deal?"

"No," said Forrest, regret in his soft voice.

You could almost see his long nose crinkle at the possibility of cutting himself in for a small percentage of such a deal.

"If you hear anything, the number is on the card."

Piron lingered in the doorway of a shop opposite, and after four minutes, Forrest shambled out of his doorway and made towards the nearest bus stop. He was obviously a man who worked hard for his money. Finding a telephone box, the detective called the office and asked for Hogg—who wished to talk about two unsavoury clients with money who had come in during Piron's absence—to come out immediately. He stood and basked in the June sun, and eventually Hogg arrived in a taxi. "I could do with a swim," he greeted Piron, which was a lie because he would have sunk like a stone and like all the citizens of North London eschewed all types of bath on principle.

"We go to Richmond, you driving, eat Maids of Honour until we are greasy, then doze in the Park until opening time. We look for a man named Fat Giles, short, pimply with a fair beard and presumably a lot of condition on him."

"Overtime?"

"Expenses which will include a cold collation, like a high class wake."

Hogg sulkily drove, and eventually, surfeited by the queer, custardy taste of the cakes, they lounged in the car, watching an old deer which sneered at them from behind some bushes.

"You think this fellow Giles is a forger?" asked Hogg.

"Forrest evidently has him on the unscrupulous list. Now I'm going to sleep for an hour."

When he woke the cakes had left a stickiness in his mouth. "I don't know where the pub is, you'll have to ask a policeman." Hogg snarled all around his blackheads, but it was not too hard to find, one of the oddments of the eighteen fifties, due for rebuilding, comfortable in a sleazy way, full of relicts, stoutly corseted widows of stockbrokers mostly.

"'Alf past eleven jobs," opined Hogg at his coarsest, "with half a bottle of gin under your belt and yer eyes half gone."

"Alcohol increases sexual desire but decreases capacity," said Piron, leading Hogg to the snack bar, buying him a cold plateful but abstaining himself.

"Not where I come from. The only legitimate births occur when they get home drunk." Hogg chose the most expensive viands, with various lecherous glances at the relicts and barmaids. Presently they sat at a table, sipping warm light ale. Why the hell the English never properly refrigerate beer, Piron never could fathom. He asked Hogg.

"Iced beer stops up the nose which is why you Yanks and also the Strines talk so funny."

Piron was about to throw the open vowels of New Zealand into the ring, when a squat, pimply fat man, well dressed but probably unwashed, entered. He was fair-headed and possessed the kind of goatee beard which should never be grown. His twinkling blue eyes, beneath shaggy brows, took it all in as he strutted towards the bar. Curiously some of the ladies smiled back at him.

Piron went to the bar with his quickly emptied glass and stood beside him. "Mr Giles?"

He had seen the reaction too many times before to be mistaken, the momentary consternation, the weight going on the back foot, then the false façade of confidence.

Bad breath struck Piron's face. "I'm Giles all right, but I don't know you."

"Bring your drink to my table. Nothing you can lose by it. On the other hand," Piron pocketed his change, "if you did not there could be unpleasantness."

"Eff you," said the fat man. Like many people of his build he was suddenly irascible, probably resulting from blood pressure and kidney disease. Nevertheless he followed Piron over.

"Mr Hogg, this is Mr Giles."

"Looks it," said Giles, who had a tendency to slobber when upset.

"Pull your pimples in," said Hogg.

"Who are you?" Giles waved his whisky-and-ginger-ale like a wand.

"Private investigator."

The pimply man thought for a minute. "And I know the dirty Scotch bastard who told you to see me, don't I?"

"You are drinking his national product, my dear boy."

"Funny man!"

"I'm only after a little info about a large quantity of reproduction silver, and I was told you are the best in the business."

Few people can dodge the direct, fulsome compliment, and Giles was no exception, even managing a rather horrible bridling expression of mock modesty. "And in that you are effing well right, cock. I won three competitions while I was still at the Tech. Of course having no cash and no business training I had to go and make the dough for others. There's a lot of jealousy, and when times got tough eighteen months ago I was about the first to get the key of the street. That's frank. I was always the man to tell the guv'nor when he was being dafter than usual and he remembered it. O' course when it came to the point, the others in the shop ran away, and the union didn't want to know about it. So now I travel for bathroom fittings and having a bit of taste and knowledge of aesthetics they value me. Why should loos be ugly, I ask?"

"I agree they are a way behind," said Piron, "but what firm finances you in this carsey caper?"

"I freelance." Giles was not very quick on the uptake.

"But leaving the pre-lavatoryite movement, what about repro silver?"

"I've made hundreds of George Three salt cellars. Good Lord! Elizabethan porringers, whatever was wanted. Occasionally from an original, more often from a series of photos. They are sold to museums, technical schools, private cits as repro. And they aren't cheap, after the capitalist has added his gouging percentage."

"Did you know a man named McGregor?"

"No." The reply was staccato and too quick.

"And you haven't worked silver for say eighteen months?"

"No. Not that I can swear to the date without looking up my cards." Giles was very much on the back foot.

Piron finished his ale, kicked Hogg under the table, and said, "Thanks, Mr Giles, it was only general background I wanted to know." They left him looking puzzled. The relicts continued drinking their gin-and-tonic.

He drove Hogg home. The weasel-faced youth said: "I didn't like the smell of it, Mr Piron. I got that certain itch."

"I am not interested in your sexual life." But Piron was worried. Hogg rarely called him 'Mr' and he himself had sensed something ugly. His assistant requested to be dropped at an address not his own, and Piron left him enquiring if Elsie was at home tonight. It was a hostel for fallen girls: Piron thought Hogg was preparing to assist in the flight.

It was ten thirty when Piron got home and June was sweet, cloying, and rather hateful. She had thrown her special goulash away at six o'clock. That she was ravenous did not matter! Piron fought back his tiredness and drove her to the most expensive of the local clubs where they had roast beef and danced until two. He supposed he could start cashing in his assurance policies, receiving back his hard-won savings in today's debased currency.

Later, in one of those bed conversations where the words echo queerly in the darkened room, as if spoken by some third party, he heard himself say: "It looks as though McGregor was in with a silver forgery racket."

"Nonsense. It looks like being a bloody life with you perpetually bleating about forgery."

In a huff, Piron turned over.

"Fine. I'll cuddle your back, but it will be rather sweaty," said June.

It was a hot night, and Piron was used to a light blanket only. He lay awake while his past life reeled by in his mind, like a drowning man's.

"Perhaps we'll live in the country," murmured June, "and you can garden on Sundays!" The sweat turned cold on Piron.

The weather, in its perfidious English way, switched during the night, and Piron, creaking out of bed to do his daily thirty push-ups, saw drizzle creeping down the window and felt the chill of cold. He lit the gas fire and settled down on the carpet, feeling that each year the push-ups became more arduous.

"You want to tuck your belly in more," said June, cocking a pretty eye over the side of the bed.

Piron gave a vulgar response, but just then the telephone extension pealed. He groaned to his feet. It was his old friend at the Yard, but speaking from his home.

"Piron, did you see that man Holy Joe, real name Forrest?"

"Yes. He put me on to a pimply artisan named Fat Giles who dribbles when enraged."

"At five o'clock this morning, Forrest got a telephone call. At six he got up, went down to the front door, opened it and was shot through the head. His wife thought it was a car back-firing and went off to sleep for half an hour. He lived in a detached house in the Streatham area. Fat Giles, did you say?"

"He frequents the Earl Gray pub at Richmond. Fair headed, pimply, bearded, broad and five feet six."

"I'll phone through. But I would like you in my office at nine thirty."

"Another killing, lover," said Piron to June, "possibly connected with McGregor."

"Oh, God," she said, "I cannot take much more violence. Don't you take holidays? Could we not clear off to Ibiza for a month?"

"That paradise of forgery?"

"We could settle for Torre and the pimps."

"I can't stand flamenco and crêpes suzette. And there are turds in the water."

"I've only seen French tourists, but if you are fussy we could make it Bournemouth. You can still get a bathchair there and an old man to push it."

"My contract specifies six weeks, expenses paid, every three years," lied Piron, "which are spent with aged parents in Grand Rapids."

"You are impossible and must meet my parents. Father could probably put you in the ladies' underwear department."

"I started life as a fitter," coyed Piron.

She swung her legs out of bed. "Bathroom first for me and I'll do your loathsome kippers."

"Don't forget the marmalade."

Piron remembered it was Sunday. June upbraided him. "I suppose you have no sense of time."

"No good woman previously to remind me. *Eheu fugaces.* What a waste of time since I was weaned and met you."

"If you want the reeking pan thrown at your head, continue in your amiable vein."

"This afternoon Regent's Park, a packet of sticky sweets, and nostalgic memories of childhood."

"I wonder your memory can stretch that far. All right, providing that you get home for lunch by one. I bought veal chops."

"Done!" said Piron.

He always found that London on a Sunday was curiously soothing, and could never understand the rush to the coast. Even Scotland Yard rusticated like a retired hangman.

You got hardened, but he winced when he saw Mrs Forrest in the old Superintendent's office.

"You know Mrs Forrest, Mr Piron," said the Super professionally.

"I know the lady, but I was not certain of her name."

She nodded, calm but red eyed.

"What is your recollection of your conversation with Forrest?"

Piron spoke for ten minutes, only adding, "I was waiting for my assistant, and Forrest came down into the street perhaps five minutes after I had."

The Super cocked an eye at Mrs Forrest, who said: "He was

always on the go, working hard to get a living. He was too good for *them*, and he never got his rights."

"He mentioned Fat Giles?"

"He knew them all, Superintendent, everybody in the trade. He was a walking encyclopaedia. Many a wealthy man goes about today from picking his brains. Fat Giles, well he is a splendid workman, but blown with whores and the drink, was well known to him. Of course, he knew everybody in the trade, having been bred to it. I heard him tell Mr Piron that Fat Giles was in the market, having got the sack when they started decreasing staff."

"Have you met Giles?"

"He came in once about a private commission my husband was handling. An unpleasant man, I thought, but then business is business and people at our scale of life cannot be choosers."

"Now, you did not go home together, I understand?"

"It was not uncommon. My husband almost worked round the clock, and he was a member of various clubs where perhaps a bit of business could be done after normal hours."

"Do you know where he went?"

"Superintendent, we were married for forty years. We took things for granted. There was not incessant small talk. I went home, washed and changed and went to a little supper party with friends a couple of blocks away. I got home at eleven and went to bed. My husband came in at around twelve. He just put the bathroom light on, undressed and washed. I said, 'All right, dear?' He said, 'Perfect' and climbed into bed. The rest you know."

"Was there anything about his manner?"

"It was dark," said Mrs Forrest, somewhat testily. Then she hesitated. "After all those years you get pretty close. He was cheerful. I thought that he saw some profit in sight."

"Had he any enemies?"

"Business gets more and more cut-throat, and Forrest was sharp. There were a few slanging matches, people calling round, but it was never fisticuffs. Had it been, I would have called the police. There was some trouble last year about an ink-pot, and a man named Firkin got rather nasty when he knew the commission

Forrest had got. But these were the trivial troubles every business man gets. My father was in skins and he had to carry a life-preserver, they got so nasty. *Caveat emptor*, he used to say, it taking two to make a bargain, and if there were threats he'd shrewdly crack them on the elbow and they shut up. But Forrest was always a man of peace with a good solicitor. He won three slander actions, settled out of court, in his time."

"We have a car to take you home," said the Superintendent.

When she had gone, he looked at Piron and sighed. "Your Fat Giles has gone into the smoke. He lodged at a small temperance hotel. At eight this morning he went out with two suitcases, and paid his bill a week in advance, saying he was going to Margate for a time. The woman who runs it thought there was a car waiting outside. I infer that he reported his encounter with you to a superior."

"And in the meantime, Forrest had been sniffing around at the superior ankles, whose owner panicked and ordered him to be knocked off," said Piron. "I do not for a moment suppose that Giles, who I judge to be craven, had anything to do with the actual killing."

"It's easy to get abroad this time of the year," said the Superintendent. "Like the Victorian villains who always 'breakfasted in Calais' after absconding with the widows' and orphans' funds. Except that Fat Giles will probably be dining in the Ramblas in Barcelona in five hours' time, beard shaved plus a false passport. Oh, yes, we've notified the ports, but at this time of the year . . ." he shrugged.

"What was the bullet?"

"A thirty-two, badly marked from the gun, which was obviously an old one of the kind which changes hands frequently. I dare say it's sunk in the drink by now, the job is highly professional. I don't like it at all."

"There is a man named Jack Prat," said Piron, "who apparently employs a hard-nosed guy known as the Dickybird."

"I've heard of both. Prat's a wheeler-dealer who dips his well manicured fingers in the fancy, semi-legal rackets. The Dickybird is a 'minder' but would use fists, feet and in last recourse a shiv.

There are not many gunmen in the country, and of those probably eighty per cent are under the lock, leaving maybe half a dozen on the street. The gun is often an amateur's standby, or let us say the semi-pro a little out of his depth. The hardened lag knows that a gun may mean fourteen extra years or more on top of the sentence. I had a frightened crook in this office a year ago—six convictions, two involving bodily violence. His wife runs a rooming house and some young fellow left behind a pistol. He was dead scared, almost on his knees to beg me to take it off him. I did"—the old Super chuckled—"in return for a bit of peaching—he was so frightened he would have turned in his own mother had not the hag been doing three years for managing a whorehouse. Now as to Forrest, we'll have to wait for an informer, but I'll bring in the Dickybird and listen to his alibi. Bringing a bloke in has its advantages because it scares his associates to the extent when they may find it advantageous to turn him in."

"Who died?" asked June, serving up the canned soup.

"A man named Forrest, a snapper-up of unconsidered trifles. I asked him who might forge old silver. He obligingly suggested a name in return for cash and was quite speedily summoned from his bed and shot with an old pistol."

June spooned in the sippets. "Sounds like a Mafia killing, if you will forgive me."

"It's a convenient bag to sweep things into. I cannot see an American gunman pumping Mr Forrest. It might be an amateur running a bit scared. In any case I saw the man who does the contracting for violence a couple of days ago and if there had been an American hit-boy around he would have mentioned it."

"Let's eat and go to the Zoo. I want to sketch the rear end of an elephant, all those baggy folds."

"Stay in and I'll pose. The beer is colder here."

"You are too skinny and sleek. I have an idea about becoming *the* elephant painter, like Stubbs and horses."

"For God's sake, he had dead ones all over the place. You bring a dead elephant here and both of you go out."

"Then take me to the Zoo."

The weather had cleared by the time they got there. Piron did not like zoos. The monkeys had human characteristics, the serpents were obviously cogitating take-over bids, and the elephants had a constipated air obviously calling for huge doses of castor oil. Fascinated by their wrinkled rears, a by-product of their physical condition thought Piron sourly, June sat down to sketch. The usual group of bystanders prepared to breathe down her neck. "They'll be bringing them out in a minute," she said, "go and watch while I sketch for half an hour."

Piron went forward, people flanking him, as the female elephants came out for their afternoon stint of duty. "Back, please," yelled a keeper. Piron felt his ankles neatly kicked from under him, and a hand propelling him from the small of his back. Amid a bedlam of yells he sprawled into the path of the leading elephant. He tried to roll, finishing breathless on his back. An inch above his face was a wrinkled, calloused foot smelling of dung.

"Steady, Beulah!" said a calm voice. The foot hesitated and froze.

Piron's training told him to lie still: some quirk reminded him that elephants loathed mice.

"Back my girl!" The elephant farted, probably with irritation flying to her bowels, but the great foot retreated. Piron scrambled to his feet. A policeman grabbed his arm.

"Pissed?"

"I tripped."

The Sergeant sniffed. "Smells like a distillery."

"I had two beers with a Yard Super and a Guinness over lunch. I'll take any test you like at my expense."

"You want to be careful, sir, they are, after all, effing animals. All right, sir."

Piron had occasionally seen the crowds round an accident case, robbing the victim of precious oxygen, occasionally sneaking his wrist watch and wallet. He saw faces round him and for a maddened minute thought of a science-fiction conspiracy, then he saw that the faces were really kind and solicitous.

"All right, old chap?" enquired a bowler hat.

" 'E tried to run at the elephint, stands to reason elephints don't like bean run at," said a product of the welfare state.

With what he was conscious was a sheepish grin, Piron mumbled something and pushed his way through the crowd. He did not see June: he wanted a drink and there were no facilities except the small hip flask of gin that he generally carried for such emergencies. He walked rapidly away, past a chimpanzee pouring tea, up a side passage and took a swig. There was a faint, fresh memory. As he had looked down, in falling, there had been a distinctive pair of shoes, cross-patterned in red. He glimpsed them now, disappearing round the corner, and followed. There was a fringe of long hair beneath a bald patch. Jay Gould? Piron slackened his pace. It seemed to be a blind alley leading to some administrative door. The building was one storey and sprawling and inside it stank of disinfectant. The nearest door along the narrow corridor had a bolt in the open position. Piron turned the handle and entered a smallish, whitewashed room. There was an odour he could not identify. In the corner another door was set with bars. He peered through and a lioness, sprawled upon a neat straw bed, peered back with a low rumble at the back of her throat. Now Piron, his left knee still bearing scars from a German Shepherd by courtesy of a dope-smuggling gang, wants no part of lions. He wondered whether the door was locked, but checked his automatic reaction to try it—that was how kids got jelly beans caught in their noses. There was no handle to the door, merely a mortice lock. Was he overwrought or was the door slightly ajar? He started to sweat and the beast, sensing fear, stirred and moved a great front paw. Piron thought there was menace in her eyes, tawny with flecks of green. He pushed against the door with his foot. Almost imperceptibly it moved.

Piron ducked so that the lioness could not see him, but smell him she could and the low rumble increased in intensity until it became the next best thing to a roar. He pondered the chance of reaching the outer door.

"What's all this?" said an irate Scots voice and a man in hospital white appeared. He seemed in an uncertain temper. "How did you get in?"

"This door's open."

"What?" The Scot pushed Piron aside and peered through the bars. The growling ceased. He eased the door open a fraction, put it back, and produced two keys to lock it.

"She's as gentle as an old sheep, unless you bloody well step on her. Gastro-enteritis—some fool throwing stale fish to her. But what's this aboot?"

"I was following somebody. The doors were open."

"This is one of the clinics we have—maximum security. There is a microphone hook-up—we heard Tessie growling so I came along. I do warn you that two armed keepers are outside and the police have been summoned."

The lioness was looking reflectively at Piron, as an angler views the one who gets away. He had never realised that lions stank, though perhaps a bit was him. Sweat made his back cold, but just then the same police sergeant strode in with portly mien.

"This fellow has been tormenting a sick lioness," said the veterinarian.

"He was at it with Beulah, the elephant, fifteen minutes ago."

"A sex maniac! We had one last year, lusting after a Spanish mountain goat," said the vet, aghast. "I know about Australians and sheep, but an elephant!"

There was the folk-lie that they possessed a pawky humour, reflected Piron groping for his wallet. The sergeant simultaneously produced a short, fat rubber club.

"Look through the wallet," begged Piron. The policeman retreated to the outer wall and popped the end of the truncheon in his mouth like a monstrous cigar. He finally stowed the contents back into the wallet. "Your credentials are O.K., Mr Piron," but having forgotten the truncheon it came out bearing his false teeth. Fortunately the floor was covered by a thick layer of sawdust, but the veterinarian's attempt to help was not appreciated.

"Argh," said the sergeant, expectorating sawdust.

Piron remembered his half-filled flask of gin. "A restorative," he urged and the sergeant gulped.

"I have no keys," the red-headed man said quickly. "You can search me. I thought I saw a suspect and followed him."

Piron had no chance to contact June. The sergeant, a reasonable man, and the veterinarian, who procured a taxi, conveyed Piron to the police station.

"Somebody tried to push you under an elephant!" said an inspector. "Now I've heard everything."

"The hook behind the ankles plus the push in the back! I suppose a pachyderm on the skull is an efficient method of dealing with anybody. Or a lion!"

"Who? You said you were swigging gin when you saw a head and a pair of shoes going round the corner."

"I was maybe five minutes behind, feeling tottery: you don't see the hard side of an elephant's paw every day."

"The doors of the infirmary are rigidly locked," said the veterinarian. "But if you could open them, it is basically a corridor with rooms off. You can walk right through and out the other end. When we bring the animals in they are generally unconscious. They are usually the smaller beasts, the lioness being an exception."

"Who has keys?" The Inspector showed interest.

"There are four sets, all under control."

"Somebody could have access to them," said Piron.

"You are suggesting that copies were made?" The veterinarian was an intelligent man.

"Of course. He saw me following and laid a pretty little quick trap. The lioness would have killed me, I suppose."

"Well, she's a wild animal. *I* can roll her over, but one prefers a keeper with a gun to be near. They smell fear, and if they do they claw but we are professionals."

"Who could have taken a copy of the keys?"

"There *you* are the professionals, gentlemen. There are two routine keys, a Yale and a mortice, requiring three turns. Of course we have part-time labour, including students, but also unskilled labour. The keys are issued very carefully. It is a situation that has never arisen, though after the Australian zoo case, where maniacs kept throwing themselves to the lions for religious motives,* we introduced maximum security, some of the Common Market protesters wishing to immolate themselves with hyenas."

"I'm afraid that natural history is a bit above my head," said the Inspector, dismally, "and I wish to put it on record that no criticism of the Common Market has been placed before me."

"Shall we leave it?" suggested Piron. "I have done no damage and I make no complaint."

"I don't want strangers wandering about the infirmary," said the vet. "The cats are not that bad, but you try to mess about with an ape with tooth-ache!"

"We'll see the locks are changed," said the Inspector. "I shall be pleased to have one of our experts advise you on alarm systems. Of course a lock is just as secure as its key."

"I follow you," said the vet. "The trouble is that we are forced to engage a certain amount of part-time labour, things being as they are. It would not be impossible for one of them to take an impression."

"You would have a record of all names for accountancy purposes," observed the Inspector with a slight groan.

"Some students volunteer their services, and one supposes that there is nothing to prevent a false name being used in the cases of those who are paid."

"I'll send somebody out to look at the records," said the Inspector.

June was home and displeased. "Where did you get to?"

"Somebody pushed me under an elephant."

* In Perth, W. Australia.

"I wish to God you did not float in a sea of infantilism."

"Then I got into a room with a lioness who was fortunately too infirm to attack me."

"I shall," she said, "lock myself in the bedroom with a Peter deVries, the lines are sharper."

She could flounce, a process accentuated by her broad hips. Piron went into the kitchen, removed his tie and opened a quart of beer, a classic American situation, he thought, but nature follows art and there was a ring of the front-door bell. Traditionally it should have been a man with a gun, but it was only Timothy Bardel leaning on a stick which was fastened to his forearm.

"You all right, Piron?"

"Why the hell should I not be all right? Come in."

Bardel limped in. "I could do with a cold beer."

Piron helped him into the kitchen and opened a bottle. Bardel looked around with an air of unease. "The children are at home, under foot and asking questions. The wife's brothers came round, both pretty tough so I can get out with an easy mind. But I don't like it, Piron: the word is about that the boys don't like you."

"They never did much," said Piron, "but who in particular?"

"Just the boys," replied Bardel, cagey.

"I am being got at, Tim," said Piron. "Somebody tried to murder me this afternoon."

"Christ!"

"I'm not important enough: it was an elephant, or the person who nearly shoved me under it."

"Is this the famous Piron persiflage, cock? If so, shove it."

"True! One Miss June Smith developed an urge to sketch elephants. A strong urge."

"Did you see who pushed you?"

"It might have been Jay Gould. I followed somebody who looked pretty like him, and blundered into an unlocked clinical room containing a sick but cantankerous lioness. I went into the first room, as it was odds-on that I should. But whoever it was had keys."

"A keeper whose wife you have seduced!"

"The only keeper who I knew kept a brothel at Las Vegas. He

was sensitive about his wife and was a very mean man as well as being a deputy sheriff. I think Miss Smith fingered me, as we say back home. One Mr Gould was Miss Smith's boy friend until recently."

"Marriage to a hard-working woman, Piron, is a man's salvation. My wife tended towards disrespect until her fourth when she realised the side her bread was buttered, so to speak."

Piron grinned. "Skipping the uxoriousness, Tim, have you any ideas?"

"At least you have her where you can keep an eye on her. Put a recorder on the phone."

"She uses a call box. A call girl!"

"Seriously Piron, she could slip arsenic into your beer. She has a wealthy dad, is an only child. Therefore she is working for love, and the man might be your Jay Gould in the role of a murderous ponce."

"I'd have sworn she wasn't, though."

"Take a man with eight children's word for it, what they will do is startling. I had some trouble with the eldest last Easter, and the wife . . ."

"Spare me, Tim, years of promiscuity are doubtless barren, but I don't have to stand anecdotes about the kids. I don't kill easy, and my grim old secretary has my reports on file."

"Hogg phoned me and told me that I am off the hook. Let it rest, return the girl and quit the case."

"And not sleep for a couple of years worrying, plus head office thinking I'm slipping?"

Bardel looked at him. "That being so, we might as well have another drink."

"We might as well go out tonight," Piron finally bellowed at the bedroom door.

There was a grumbling noise.

"And I want the goddamned loo," howled Piron. It opened off

the bedroom. He fretted for ten minutes, when the door opened and June appeared, immaculately groomed. Sniffing, she said "Beer! I shall go and help myself."

"Where shall we go? Make it fast for reasons of state."

"I know a club with super fish and an adequate dance floor. The price will ruin you and serve you right. Keep sober! Don't drink the after-shave."

The loo had women's drip-dry undies hanging in the shower recess, noted Piron sourly.

He showered, ducking his head to avoid a dangling bra and a pair of fishnet stockings, and put on his best suit.

"The rising, though elderly executive to a T," quipped Miss Smith, putting down her beer glass.

"I shaved my chest and deodorised, lover."

"We'd better taxi, it might be a breaky-leg evening. I feel in champagne mood. I shall look the part, sweet innocence squired by a bored roué."

"As long as the club does not have elephants."

When her brow wrinkled she looked much older. "What the hell is all this jazz about elephants?"

"As long as they are white elephants I don't mind. The black, wrinkled variety I do not much care for."

"Get a cab, racist."

Piron could never really understand night boxes. They came and they went, and the more crowded the more successful. June's choice was small, and Piron had a nodding acquaintance with some of the patrons. It was superb fish, good drink, and a six-piece combo plus an unintrusive thrush. In a welcome interval, Piron sat in silence. The conversation had died in one of the verbal cul-de-sacs with which life is filled.

He stared at the ceiling: there was a prickling on the back of his neck. He swung round. Smartly clad in a blue suit was Jay

Gould, talking to a nondescript young woman at the small bar.

"Your friend Gould is on the scene," he said.

"Jay," she craned round. "Yes, but of course he does decor work for these places. You have got to alter incessantly or the crowd gets bored. He has a talent for it." Her voice was very cool. "But why the obsession about Jay? He had nothing to do with McGregor's death. As you know I'm a hair-trigger sleeper and he was in my bed. When the police knocked, I just saw them at the door. Jay went down the stairs and out, discreetly, four hours later."

"He had a key?"

"I cannot remember. He might have had one to the street door—we were all careless with keys and I personally had four cut—but not, I think, to the flat itself. Your persistent sleuth-ness is trying, my dear. I always wondered what being married to a bobby must be like: how could you cuckold a cop?"

"With the Superintendent, though I knew of a Police Chief who dropped his badge on the bedroom floor. It had to be expensively hushed up."

"Jay is not a man of violence: he has a horror of blood, liable to faint at a cut finger."

"I might take your word for it: cutting throats entails a certain temperamental hardness. Poisoners are easy men, bland and soft and subtle."

"I think we'd better have another bottle of wine, something white."

The waiter sold them three pounds' worth of hock.

Jay Gould had disappeared. Piron ordered a coffee and presently they went home.

It was three in the morning when the stomach cramps hit him. In spite of her protestations, the final brandy had reduced June to sound sleep.

Piron's doctor lived a block away, so he merely put on pants, shirt and slippers and shuffled away. The night was hot, but the muscular spasms continued. A Scot of the old school, the doctor is inclined liberally to prescribe the clyster: on the other hand he does not mind getting up at three in the morning to administer the stomach pump. Piron lay supine while an injection went into his arm.

"Not fatal, Piron," said his friend. "At least I don't think so. A pity, because the State pays me for issuing a death certificate. But somebody slipped you something nasty, enough to keep you in bed unless I had emptied your gut. I suppose I should report it."

"I would rather you did not, Fred."

"I'll put it down as suspected fish-poisoning, but you know it was not that. I can tell you from the nasty evidence that it was not in the deadly class and you'll be all right tomorrow, though if you had delayed it might have been semi-serious."

Piron went home with two boxes of pills. June was moaning faintly in her sleep. The doctor had specified no alcohol: Piron went into his living-room and read, half comprehending the words.

In spite of summer time, dawn was coy and when some light came through the window Piron awoke from half-sleep, his eyes smarting. He went back to the bedroom.

June was staring at the ceiling.

"I have a hangover," she said, "and I had a beastly dream that you had gone."

"Only with the wind, dear, saved by stomach pump at the bell." He felt weak but surprisingly hungry.

"What for breakfast—eggs?"

"Scrambled but massively plentiful," answered Piron.

The stomach pump had done its doughty work and Piron noshed a three-egg dish with bacon, replenishing.

He ate in silence, while June had aspirin and black coffee. Whatever it was must have been in the final brandy. Most poisons and emetics do not dissolve in anything but high-grade spirit.

"I should go and see my mother."

"Luxuriate among the fleshpots."

"No need to be insulting, Piron. She tries to diet, though not often, and Father's ulcers keep him bone thin."

Piron left for his office before she had dressed. Hogg had arrived early. His predilection for the wives of night-shift workers made him an admirable employee in that direction. He was shaving with Piron's electric razor, a shuddersome thought.

"Me own has bust," he said calmly, "and it started cutting through the pimples instead of gliding over like."

"Get a move on, we are going to Frippingham."

"Trouble?" Hogg peered into the mirror as though he liked what he saw.

"Jay Gould. I got pushed under an elephant yesterday and then somebody slipped me something unpleasant at a night club."

Hogg switched off the razor. "I told you no good would come of this caper, Mr Pee. Tim Bardel is willing to cry quits. Pushed under an elephant, I never heard of such a thing, though there was a girl I knew who sat on a scorpion when taken short in Andalucia and was never the same again!"

"Somebody wants me off the scene. Gould has not the stomach for direct violence: pushing under elephants and slipping things into brandy is another matter."

"Carnt you handle him yourself if he's a patsy? I got two chambermaids to see about the divorce evidence."

Piron knew that his assistant liked interviewing chambermaids about adultery, leeringly hinting at reconstructing the evidence. He said, sharply, "I'll want a witness."

"Putting it plain, you'll knock him about and I'll perjure that he attacked you."

"Control yourself, Hogg."

"I don't mind as long as the monthly bonus is all right."

"We upright Americans disdain the effete corruption of Europeans."

"At least we put it into the bank and not shoe-boxes."

"As you wear the original contents until they stink, there are not the clean, hygienic shoe-boxes around. Will you drive? After a session at the end of the clyster, I want no close acquaintance with machinery."

"I'll hire a car, boss, it'll be quicker than by the old crate." Hogg drives very fast, his face contorted by agony and emnity.

* * *

Gould had a chaste brass plate outside the ground-floor door of a duplex. There was no spy-hole and he rashly swung the door open far enough for Piron's strong bony finger to probe his midriff. "Throw me under elephants, lover-boy!" growled the red-headed man, entering, with Hogg discreetly behind him.

Breathing gustily, Gould turned to run, but Piron took him by the elbows. Most of the duplex was one studio, its furniture probably picked up by Gould from his peers. Piron sat Gould on the big circular bed with its attendant mirrors and built-in hi-fi.

"Son," he said, "when did you work at the Zoo? And do not lie because it will be on the easy side to get an identification!"

"I did work there, part time, four years ago when I was doing a course in wood-carving," said Gould, obviously thinking fast.

"I'll smack you in the mouth if you get smart." Piron jutted his chin, and dug his fingers into Gould's biceps. It was standard, brutal procedure and Hogg came in to bat. "Let me 'ave 'im to take to the boys, guv!, so they can do things to him," he said in a horrible, menacing whine. He outlined in detail the strange things the boys would do before throwing Mr Gould into twelve feet of Thames mud. Gould turned green.

"Now," said Piron, on page two of the scenario, "that means expense and I'd rather do it here, but it could be done reasonably by a quiet, cosy little chat, like all friends together."

"What do you want?"

Piron sat down beside him. "Let's be buddy boys. Who got you to trip me under the elephant?"

"A phone call. A hundred quid."

"And the lioness?"

Gould remained at a loss. "Hold 'im down while I give him the old massage," begged Hogg, producing a cigarette lighter.

"I don't like the smell of scorched pig," said Piron, "at least not now, though I could change my mind. Come on, now, who was it!"

Gould's mouth was dry. He croaked, "There will be a hundred quid left at a club I know. It was a voice. You don't give that kind of voice lip."

"And how did you know I was going to be around the elephants?"

"June Smith. She telephoned and gave me hell. I said 'Let's meet on Sunday' and she said 'On Sunday I will be sketching elephants' arses at the Zoo.' Q.E.D."

"And the night club?"

"She always goes there. A habituée, stoking up on the *sole caprice* when some sucker is paying to lay her. I was merciful, it could have been thallium, instead of the little arsenic derivative they give difficult customers."

"Lend me the cigarette lighter, Hogg."

"Wiv pleasure, guv'nor."

"I'm telling you the truth," said Gould, pulling himself together.

"Who owns the club?"

"A syndicate headed by Jack Prat. It's expensive, but good value, and they watch out for customers who might want some action in the gambling way. If so they provide a hire car out to Jack's casino-club. There are a good many similar operations."

"Did Prat know about the arsenic?"

"No. I slipped it in when the bartender was pouring it."

"In the brandy?"

"Yes."

Piron smacked him across the mouth. "There were two brandies, my old dear. I had one and June Smith had one."

"I gave the waiter a quid to give you the doped one."

"You're a liar. You gave the dose to Smith and she put it in my brandy. She was away ten minutes in the ladies': you could not see the entrance from where we were seated.

"The truth's not in you." Piron towered over him and looked down with spiteful eyes. "If you get in my road again you'll never forgot it."

Inspector Feld was in his office, squinting at the usual mass of paper work. Piron introduced Hogg who made his usual unfavourable impression.

"Did you know that Jay Gould was in June Smith's bed when McGregor was killed?"

Feld shrugged. "Do you want to reopen the case? I thought that Joyningstowe was the tailor-made culprit."

"The supposition originally was that McGregor had opened his shop and gone to sit in his office until Bardel entered by the street door and cut his throat. The second theory was that Joyningstowe had come down the back stairs and committed the crime. The latter has its points—he could have cleansed himself of any blood on his return to his apartment. On the former theory, the killer would run a risk entering by the shop door, but far less if he went in by the entrance to the apartments. The tenants were not early risers, they had no sense of urgency to be up and about. He or she could have gone to the first landing, along the corridor and down the back stairs. Before he went out the same way he could have snibbed back the front-door lock and pulled the supporting bolts."

"God knows why you persecute me!" said Feld. "But the knife was in the shop. How did your killer get out there, take the knife, and return to the office? That is what bothers me regarding the Joyningstowe theory, unless he came down to the street and entered the shop door."

"How many knives were there in the set?"

"Three."

"One for meat, one for poultry—and the other?"

"You mean?"

"That the killer saw a set of carving knives in the shop and brought a similar one. He erred in leaving a smear of blood on it, but it was a damned good idea."

"A minute." Feld took up his red handset. Eventually he said, "You specialise in making me look an idiot. Forensic say that the blood-stained knife did not match the set: the haft is ivory, the others mother-of-pearl. Nobody thought anything of it."

"Snegg has an inventory, though I suppose they were just listed as a set of knives. You could try to trace it, but the London street markets are loaded with old knives: I bought a Chinese chicken chopper in Portobello Road a month ago."

"You realise that you reopen suspicion upon your client, Bardel?"

"I open suspicion on the tenants, Inspector. If I am correct somebody supplied a key."

"You keep on hinting at Gould. What motive?"

"Money. If you get a complaint from him that I smacked him over the chops, Mr Hogg will depose that he flew at me like a wildcat and I merely fended him off."

Feld yawned. "You're talking to a copper. I know you are lying but could not prove it."

"Can I teach Granny to suck eggs?"

"If you keep on this particular granny will be sucking eggs—the cheapest available—on point duty up in Nottingham."

"Check the knife, bear down on Gould, and watch Snegg."

"You're saying that somebody lent or gave a key to the killer."

"That is the premise."

"Miss Traylor," fairly groaned Feld, "said she heard footsteps outside her door, but she is so discredited as a witness... And then there is the shop opposite, a high-class delicatessen where the staff comes in at seven thirty. There was a boy cleaning windows and he says he saw no one going into the shop, nor any activity as he remembers. His angle of vision did not properly cover the entrance to the house, but he had the impression somebody went in. I say 'impression' and it's not something which would stand up to cross-examination. It will be far better if we peg it on to old Joyningstowe: nevertheless I will routinely pursue the course you suggest, which having said I suggest a sandwich and a pint at the pub."

Feld was good company and even, with a side-long glance at Piron, managed a laugh at the corrupt limerick produced from Hogg's vast repertoire of the same.

"We were a bit curious *in re* the lady," he said slyly over his second bitter, "but we understand that she has taken up new quarters."

"No motive. Drawn—into my humbler quarters—but the eye apple, or at least the heir and assign, of a millionaire daddy."

"Leopold and Loeb had millionaire daddy-os."

"But not elderly Jewish antique dealers as their victims," protested Piron. "Freud himself would be stuck for a sexual reason. Vice versa, yes, Vienna was filled with murderous old antique dealers, but it's young boys and girls who get done in or molested."

"Well, Mr Piron, we find curious happenings in police work. I know that sex is number one—and I don't suppose St Paul knew the work he was giving us—but money is the second key, ask any newspaper editor. One just wonders."

"She's a greedy bint," said Hogg.

"People *are* greedy," the Inspector massaged his face.

Piron ordered a second round of the excellent rare-beef sandwiches.

"Ta," said the Inspector, spooning the green mustard over the top.

"I'd like to get Bardel completely cleared," said Piron.

"There's no such thing," said the Inspector. "'Not Guilty' does not mean 'innocent', and we are none of us unguilty."

"I bloody well am," said Piron, recognising the symptoms. "My virginity was snatched from me by a prurient nurse at the age—mine—of eleven; I have led a God-fearing life, realising that one's virginity, as it were, cannot be handed back. But I voted for Mr Nixon, and am a practising Elk."

"You are a frivolous man," said Feld, "but there is a little book you should read which explains the problems of today."

"The one about the pill," said Hogg sagely. "Little girls learn it on their mother's knee, Inspector, along with the law of alimony. I sometimes blench at what I see in earning a modest living. The other night..."

"Hogg!" interposed Piron. "We should be away."

The Inspector was looking at Hogg with acute dislike. "We must not let the degrading things we see degrade us, Mr Hogg. My father, before he retired, was a prison warder in charge of the condemned cell. He said it was wonderful to see the uplift and spiritual resignation as the hour of eight a.m. came near, though of course regulations insisted he had to bind them, but he privately opined that the Mercy we can all sustain would have placed them on the trap without a struggle."

"Like the Jews in Belsen," snarled Hogg, who had sneakily ordered a double-whisky chaser.

"We are not talking of Jews," said the Inspector distastefully, "though I find them law-abiding. I trust I am not talking of your religion, Mr Piron."

"I only eat Jewish, being a fervent Christian."

"I can see, Mr Piron that I am beating against a stone, but if you ever need Guidance . . ."

"A rum fellow," judged Hogg, as Piron drove.

"They sometimes get that way in police work," said Piron. "You've got to find some raft to anchor your conscience to. Sometimes it's drink, sometimes it's women, and sometimes little esoteric books."

"They'd be dirty photos?"

"I despair of you, Hogg."

"You are an idealist, Mr Pee. Take old Bardel with eight nippers eating him out of house and home—idealism was the root of it all and now he hasn't an arse-piece, hardly, to his pants."

"I am childless, Hogg."

"A fault of the genes, sir, not for want of trying."

"To come back to your favourite point, Hogg, I wonder about McGregor and women. Jews generally prefer a family life. Get round to Somerset House."

"Surely, guv, she'd have been round to the Executors like a bloody bee round a honey pot. You know what women are, the world owes them a living. I was serious about a girl last Christmas, but then the penny dropped. She carried on about wall-to-wall carpet, central 'eating and deep freeze. I thought her charms justified that, but then she upped and said she would give up her twenty-five-nicker-a-week job in the furniture factory. I sent her off."

"He could have made a cash settlement, a lot of people do. McGregor had a run of luck twenty years or so ago. If his marriage had gone on the rocks he might have paid off."

Piron dropped Hogg at Knightsbridge and drove to his apartment. He entered with caution, something he had not done for years, whipping back the door and listening. There was a smell of stew. June was eating in the kitchen.

"Eaten, Piron?"

"Sandwiches with a copper and my man, Hogg."

"Joy!"

"I suppose Gould was on the blower. I had occasion to smack him round the chops."

"You will see that I'm just starting to eat Irish stew. I left it simmering while I went to see my mother who is worried about trade unionism and Father's growing deafness and senility. The other day he granted an increase to the staff and is being threatened with a gaol sentence by the powers-that-be. Gould did not phone and you should not have smacked him."

"He said that you told him you were going to the Zoo yesterday."

"After you had tortured him!" Her whiteness accentuated her auburn hair.

"He scares easy. The story was that I had to be put away for a bit and nobody was worried about how."

"I'll tell you this, Piron, I did tell him I was going to the Zoo." She pushed her plate away. "And I'll throw in a bonus. At the Club last night I saw him outside the ladies'. He said you were in for it, but if I poured a little vial of stuff into your brandy, you would fall asleep and I could get a couple of waiters to put you into a cab."

"But I did not fall asleep."

"It was one of his cruel jokes."

"I went and had the clyster around three a.m. It was arsenical: had it killed me it would have been you who did the forty years."

"I did not know, Piron, I swear I did not know."

"Then do not worry your pretty head. Though if Mr Gould phones pray tell him he is in dire jeopardy."

He went to the office. "An urgent letter, by a delivery boy," announced his grim old secretary. "I thought it better to keep it for you in person." Piron always thought she did not approve of Hogg, though it was difficult to fathom her thoughts.

It was from his friend on the technical magazine. A short covering letter introduced a reply to his advertisement. It was from a Mr Charles Savory, an American citizen, staying at the Madeleine Hotel. He was empowered to sell a collection of rare old silver for two hundred thousand pounds, but it would have to be purchased in one lot. It represented a bargain, presented by a client who had found it necessary to liquidate some of his assets. Any professional appraisal would be welcomed.

Outside the office door were a series of brass plates, for 'front' purposes. Similarly six telephone lines existed and were duly listed in the telephone directory. Piron chose 'Birmingham Brass Investors', and summoned his secretary. "Mr Savory," she said at last—the Madeleine was very discreet—"this is Birmingham Brass Investors. Sir James Gackerley is on the line."

"Gackerley speaking," said Piron in his best British. "Aim ver' interested in yer proposal, though one would have to have one's man to look at the stuff."

"We have had it appraised," said Savory, in Middle West. "It is worth at least three hundred thousand, a wonderful hedge the way West politics are going."

"Clean?"

"Of course, Sir James. Some of it might not have paid Customs originally, but that is old water under an old bridge. A silver bridge, heh! heh!"

"One prefers not to joke when one is discussing money of this magnitude."

"Quite, Sir James, but sometimes a bit of wit eases the conversation."

"I'll come over presently and see it."

"Oh, it's in a vault, Sir James, but we could maybe reach a climate of discussion, currency, etcetera."

"It would not be Swiss your client is requiring?"

"Well, of course, the client would like Swiss, Kraut or Jap, as dear old Spiro would say. But something could be worked out, I'm sure."

"I'll be over."

Piron's secretary removed the tape-recorder extension from underneath the handset.

The Madeleine was oldish, expensive, the scene of many of Piron's divorce assignments, served recherché little meals in the private suites, and stank in its upper regions of bath essence. They did not like publicity at the Madeleine, and apart from upper-bracket whoring, many a take-over, union or political deal had been concluded in its dismal Bloomsbury environment. The desk clerks were new to him—they changed often at the Madeleine, improving themselves to the rank of gigolo or ponce.

"I have an appointment," said Piron. One of the clerks went behind the sound-proofed barrier and telephoned.

"Horace!" The 'boy' had probably been a reasonably good lightweight boxer, "take this gentleman to suite forty."

Piron slipped Horace a suitable gratuity as they went up in the lift. "An American gennelman you wanna see", said the 'boy' and Piron wondered if he discerned a word of warning.

In the eventuality there was no need. It was a nice, scented pad: years of distressing experience warned Piron that, on his discreet tap, a girl had locked herself in the bathroom. Mr Savory was short and tubby. Piron recognised him from New York and Chicago days. A skilled wheeler-dealer, Savory, who went by various names, would procure for you an expensive lady, a hot car, the entrée to a gambling school, forged documents of any description. Piron saw his face freeze, as he shut the door to the suite. "I know you," said Savory.

"Mutual," said Piron. "I should have guessed: you go in for herbal names. Mr Mace you called yourself in that reclaiming used car oil racket ten years ago."

"Racket! It worked, but the reclaimed oil did not work," protested Savory. "And talking of assumed names . . ."

"Let's have a drink and be sociable," begged Piron.

"I don't see why I should stand dicks whisky at the price the limeys charge," grumbled Savory as he poured, while Piron sat on one of the over-stuffed chairs.

"We Americans have to drink together."

Savory said some unpleasant things about his homeland, in which Piron knew he had achieved free lodging for seven years in a waggishly named 'house of correction'.

"Dartmoor is worse, but only just," said Piron, "and no actual rapes occur in the subway. But why, dear friend, this silver thing?"

"I'm broke, Piron, down to my last thousand bucks. It's a long story but there it is. I got this chance to sell a great parcel of old silver, perfectly legit."

"Who is the vendor?" asked Piron.

"The deal is that it is secret."

"There was a dealer named McGregor who had his throat cut."

"Are you playing tricks?"

"I'm levelling. He was implicated in a transaction remarkably like yours."

Savory put his drink down. "I'm not a man who likes violence, Piron. You know that."

"You'd sell your wife for ten dollars, you dirty little bastard!"

"Say fifty, you've been away for a long time. But I've never raised my fist to anybody except a woman, she being on the frail side at that. Let me think."

Piron sensed rather than heard the bathroom door open.

"Thinking cost us twelve thousand dollars in Paris. I'll do the thinking, Charlie." She was small and nut brown from the sun, but perhaps Mexican. The gun was one of the low-calibre jobs with a soft bullet which spreads on impact.

"I am clean, obedient and love you and Charlie, ma'am," said Piron, very still.

"I've heard of you, Piron, as a third-class louse. You busted a friend of mine."

Piron thought. He had the idea it might have been a whorehouse specialising in blackmail and nut-brown ladies.

"At that," the woman said, "you have more brains than Charlie who buys non-existent property. The sucker!"

"Now, Valerie!"

"Shut your gob, Charlie." She sat down. "Make no mistake about it, Piron, I can't stand the rough stuff any more and if you try to beat us up I'll cut it short—through your navel."

"Nerve gone?" asked Piron.

"I got my first beating at thirteen," she said. "Fifteen years later I decided enough was enough. Now you know."

"I promise you no violence."

"About that time, Piron, I got smart about taking a man's word on anything."

"I only want a deal. A man named McGregor had a load of old silver to sell. He was negotiating with an operator, one Jack Prat. McGregor got his throat cut ear to ear, as the books say."

"We're out, Charlie," she said bitterly. "I can always go back to whoring and you can work as a shill. I'll put the gun away, Piron." She stuck it in the drawer of the little writing-desk.

Charlie asserted himself. "We had a run of bad luck. The property deal looked all right, but you know what these Spanish property deals are like. Sure, there was the land but no water and electricity for miles, plus the wind screeching like an evangelist in full cry. I bought it from the mayor—you'd think mayors were honest."

"Only in our country, where political probity pervades."

"For Christ's sake," said the woman, "get up and do your patter, if you have to. Prat engaged us. He's paying for the suite: we do a sideline in steering people to the gambling. My knees are sore with inadvertently stumbling into visiting firemen outside the American Consulate. On balance it's harder than whoring and far more boring."

"I don't get this," said Piron. "Prat was supposed to be the buyer."

"Maybe he's bought and reselling. If we get the customer we process him and phone Prat."

"Is the stuff genuine?"

"How should I know?" asked Valerie. "Heyho, silver! The buyer can provide his own expert."

"Maybe something phoney about the expert," said Charlie. "Prat gave me a list of guys who are experts. I would try to steer the buyer to one of them."

"Have you got the list? I'll take a shorthand note."

After a side-glance, Savory rather miserably produced from his wallet a list of eight typewritten names. Piron recognised one name, a gentleman of eighty-five summers who still owned and operated a small art shop in a condition of beneficient senility. The others meant nothing.

"Piron," said Valerie, "we are in deep waters we know nothing about. We'd rather you kept your trap shut and there's no money, no cash, only kind." She sighed. "You look the age when you prefer a mature woman."

"My trap is so shut that there are times when I can't even take my bread and milk. And no kind."

"Thank God for that, I can't stand red-headed men. I was preparing to offer you Charlie." She grinned, a saucy little woman.

"We might as well finish the whisky as Prat is paying for it," said Piron, and Savory poured with fawning alacrity.

"I suppose we'd better get packing," the woman said.

"You can stay with it," said Piron. "You are committing no crime, and I certainly will not mention this confidential interview to anyone."

"Prat will know you've been here," said Charlie Savory, whose instinct always was to run. "The desk clerks . . . well, I know the type. One or more would be reporting to Jack Prat."

"When I go, phone Prat. Tell him I came round, but you clammed up."

"We'll milk it for another month, Charlie, then back to Las Vegas and the cowboys," decided Valerie.

Charlie looked far from keen.

Piron said, "I told you there was a killing, but at least one of you seems formidable. I'd keep inside."

"We haven't the dough to go out," the man said bitterly.

"I'd dispose of that pistol, but if you smell trouble, phone me. I'll leave my card."

"Deeper in and deeper," said Hogg, with whom Piron discussed the visit. "A 'ore, is she?" he remarked with interest. "What does she charge?"

"She offered it free."

"No wonder you look clapped out, guv."

"I refused it," said Piron haughtily.

"You oughta buy some of these afrodaisyacs," said Hogg sceptically. "You're not gettin' any younger. I do not like anything I hear about Prat but I suppose we had better brace him. No good phoning: he would not open the door. Better get Hymie: if you turn it down for free you're in no condition to fight."

On reflection Piron did get Hymie, who is five feet six and nearly as broad. Hymie can smash a table with one chop from a ham-like hand and his reflexes are lightning fast. His living comes from guarding divorce detectives from the enraged assaults of paramours and an occasional push in the face from the ladies. He has not a brain in his head, spending his non-working hours vacantly consuming tea in a St Martin's Lane caff and boggling at comic strips. "I can take the man, Hymie," said Piron, "but he might have some nasty boys."

"You want them hurt, like a hospital?"

"That might be as well."

"It's double rate for really hurting."

"Fine," said Piron.

It was the Dickybird who answered their ring, and at Piron's nod Hymie went about the task of spraining his back.

"Hold it," said Piron, as Jack Prat appeared. He did not want witnesses.

"What the devil is this?" asked Prat, but smoothly as if under the impression that the Dickybird's habitual method of progression was by crawling along the floor.

"You've been telling untruths, you naughty boy," said Piron.

"I've got guests." Piron heard Hogg's adenoidal breathing over his shoulder.

"So you've got more? I heard you are selling old silver."

"Now," said Prat, "suppose you and your boys take a thousand in notes."

"Slow, sure but honest," said Piron, watching Hymie stamp on the Dickybird's hand and kick the knife away.

"Just take it easy, friend," said Hymie in his flat voice. "We don't want no trouble, but I could take your kneecaps off easy."

"I think I'd better get the police," said Jack Prat.

"I'm sure the Dickybird would make an admirable witness."

"I and associates acquired some silver," said Prat. "No law against it."

"Forged silver?"

"I know nothing of its provenance. There are experts who will examine it."

"There are skilled silversmiths. One died in Portugal recently."

"Piron," said Prat, "pull your bib out. This one"—he gestured to the Dickybird who was now holding on to the wall—"is third string. I could bring in the first league."

"I don't like that, mister," said Hymie, intent but puzzled. "Do I do something nasty to him, Mr Piron?"

"I don't think so, Hymie. Mr Prat is a great big bag of wind and he'd burst."

"It's stalemate, Piron," said Prat. "I have three people in the sitting-room and if you touch me I'll yell." The Dickybird slid down the wall into a sitting position.

They paid off Hymie and dropped him in St Giles' Circus, leaving him staring around vacantly as if he had not seen the place thousands of times.

" 'E knows his work and warms to it like a craftsman," said Hogg. "It's a pity that he hasn't got a square inch of brain."

"We are damned lucky that he hasn't: he'd make a sizable kind of crim if he had the faintest intelligence."

"Before we get back, we might see Mrs McGregor. June Adelaide Elizabeth, née Poe. She is listed in the phone book in one of the own-it-yourself high-rise flats a hundred yards away. It took me two hours and three taxis to sort out." Hogg smirked with the certainty of a man who has fiddled the expense account.

The woman who answered the door was a large, dyed blonde with a twinkling look of humour.

"We're investigating Julius McGregor's death," said Piron.

"I only read of it, but the coffee is perking so you may as well come in."

It was a combined kitchen and living area which smelled pleasantly of good coffee.

She poured out three cups and they sat down. "I had not seen Julius for twelve years and I shall not attend his funeral, not from callousness but because some memories are better not revived. I married him in 1950. I was a divorcee. God knows what happened. I *liked* Julius. On the other hand I like theatre and music and dancing, and Julius didn't, so it didn't work; a no-go area. I was not greedy, having money of my own, and we made a settlement."

"What kind of man was he?"

"You know his history?"

"Fairly well."

"He could have become introvert or extrovert: it was the former. He thought of nothing but business after the first burst when he courted me—we met at the Victoria and Albert because I had an interest in embroidery. So after two years I gave him grounds to divorce me—easier that way, British judges being hard on fallen ladies. I have never remarried and have pleasant thoughts of Julius."

"Any thoughts on who killed him?"

"Who kills anyone? There was a self-righteous better-than-thou streak in Julius, but apart from his dullness that was his only fault. He was dead honest within the essential framework of dealing, physically he would not have hurt a fly. I suppose there was some money motive."

She thought for a moment. "He specialised in antique silver. It was something of an obsession. I don't know, but I would judge that he developed into a world-class expert on the subject. When you have been pushed around and bullied like poor Julius you need something of permanent value to hang on to."

"Mrs McGregor," said Piron, "I would like you seriously to reconsider your statement that you had no contact with Julius for that number of years, because my appraisal of him is as a warm-hearted man in his way and I think you are an understanding woman."

She did not like it and sat for a long minute in thought. "I do not want to get involved. My life is my own."

"Julius's life was his own."

"You are a swine."

"I just want the truth."

"We had some business dealings. I never saw Julius, of that I assure you, but we had a mutual accountant and an occasional phone call. Pure business: he occasionally wanted money for a deal and he paid good interest. At the moment I probably owe the Estate six hundred pounds, but there is money owing to me which may cover it. The accountant will cope."

Piron finished his coffee and thanked her. He and Hogg walked to the taxi rank. "Lying, weren't she?" asked Hogg clinically. "They tend to leer and waggle their 'ands about when they're lying and that is what she was doing."

"I don't like the way the expenses are mounting up," said Piron, "otherwise we might get someone to shadow her."

"I'll get a spot check done, Mr Pee, like phoning her up at all hours, plus a girl I know who solicits orders for a book club. Won't cost much in the long run and we just might get a lead."

V

June Smith had been very subdued, thought Piron as he donned his smartest grey suit the next morning. Essential pessimism told him that when women are in that state they are Planning Something. He had been wary as he ate his cereal—a ghastly compound which claimed to loosen the bowels and probably did—and chewed bacon and eggs which he privately considered the English incapable of cooking. However there had been no cunning, oblique conversational ploys, and they kissed in silence before he made his way to Scotland Yard.

The old Superintendent was flanked by an inspector and a senior sergeant. Piron had taped his comments while he was waiting and it was merely a question of switching on the player, a useful technique in police work.

"Mm," said the Super after it had come to an end. "And it was so handy to have pinned the whole boiling on to old Joyningstowe. Feld telephoned me, a bod named Jay Gould complained you had forced your way in and knocked him about."

"I have a witness to say I did not!"

The Super twinkled and yawned. "I once inadvertently tripped and trod on the face of Snyder, the child-killer, and had two sergeants to vouch that it was an accident. However, Snyder was so upset he told us where he had buried the last little body. I cannot encourage such methods in my exalted position. Feld is worried. We cannot afford to have a skilled throat-cutter around. I was consulting our librarian, there are various allusions to the art of throat-cutting in old travel books: about the Borneo headhunters for example. There is a certain art to it, but I suppose one could practise on a cushion. This man, Prat, for instance, once worked the liners as a card-player, one of a party of three, until that trade died out, and is much travelled. You learn strange things if you travel a lot."

Piron knew that the chauvinistic old gent had never made any excursion other than a hurried, timorous trip to Paris to pick up an absconding solicitor. He said, "I do not see Prat soiling his hands."

"The Dickybird is in the clear," replied the Super. "He was in an all-night poker school, with four Danish tourists who got skinned. The evidence is conclusive. I wish to God," he moaned, "that McGregor had cut his own throat."

"Even the English constabulary could hardly imagine a person administering such a gash," said Piron sourly.

"Suppose that McGregor had the silver cached away," said the Super. "In some obscure warehouse under an assumed name, for instance. Prat could have had him killed, or done the job himself, and taken collection of the loot himself."

"Evidence is that it is forged."

"Which is immaterial," said the Super. "A colleague told me that there is virtually no difference between genuine old silver and expertly contrived copies."

"The only evidence that McGregor was offering silver for sale is, at final analysis, that of Jack Prat."

"In the kind of case that this is, these things are hard to pick," said the Super. "Why should Prat lie?"

"The man, Forrest, who was shot not long after McGregor died, might have been on to something. Prat has connections. I judge he'd have your throat cut with a charming smile."

"Funny how eighty per cent of my customers have charming smiles," said the Super. "I got my daughter married to a man with warts, a squint and a constipated look and they've never had a cross word."

"I'm going down to Frippingham," said Piron.

"Everything there is being handled competently."

"It's just a hunch," said Piron.

They watched his tall, lank body go through the door.

"You'd better get down to Frippingham," the Super told his two assistants. "Cover him tightly."

"He sounds like a blow-hard," opined the Sergeant.

"He is capable, but more to the point, lucky," said his superior.

"More important, we want the credit. These agencies skim off the cream and don't do us any good."

"Ar," said the Sergeant, a notoriously unlucky and envious man.

Piron first called on Tim Bardel, now on his feet, but with his crutch under one shoulder.

"We'll clean this up, Tim," he said.

"It's as clean as ever it will be," said Bardel, "leaving the usual indelible stain. Bardel is all right, but . . . It's hard when you have eight mouths to fill, not counting the wife, with prices getting what they are. Cod is what we have on Fridays and last week it cost . . . oh, well, I suppose it doesn't interest a gay bachelor."

"The other day you were advocating marriage."

"I must have forgotten the price of cod," groaned Bardel. "Father Murphy says that I shall go to my Reward, but it would be my luck to receive a couple of tons of cod, which I detest."

"He might just make it smoked salmon! But, seriously, Tim, the answer to your immediate problem lies at Frippingham. There might be something you forgot. It sometimes happens."

Bardel sat down clumsily. "It occurred to me last night. I might have heard a door close."

"Where?"

"I suppose the door from his office to the private stair. Yet, you know, I could not swear to it."

"It makes the time factor narrow," said Piron, "unless . . ."

"Unless . . . you mean somebody in the house!"

"It must be, I think. It is an old place fundamentally, with God knows how many closets and disused storerooms disguised by a modern façade. And then there were the tenants. I'm afraid I cannot see Joyningstowe, which leaves Miss Traylor, whose brain is partially softened, old Snegg, the Scots dominie, June Smith and Jay Gould who was in her bed at that moment."

"Women don't often use a knife," said Bardel.

"They may at a pinch."

"And the motive?"

"McGregor knew the silver was forged—a slip somewhere. It is difficult for a forger not to make a slip, as you know. Sometimes his eyes deceive him, sometimes it is a kind of black-out."

"I remember an alleged eighteenth-century sketch of the Royal coaches," said Bardel, "and there were a lot of them. If you looked through a glass you saw that one of them, for children, had a pneumatic tyre!"

The telephone rang and the call was for Piron.

In his horrible voice Hogg said, "Mrs McGregor called and has decided to tell what she did not the other day."

"I thought she was holding out!"

"McGregor did not trust anybody," said Hogg. "A bloke who's seen his world collapse doesn't trust anybody: they are all like boils on his arse. However you can't be an island."

"For Christ's sake do not turn literary on me," snarled Piron. "Sell it to *Reader's Digest* with the addition of copious references to our Maker and the working of adrenal glands."

"You will 'ave your little giggle, Mr Pee," said Hogg. "But the lady said she would drop a certain something in to our office. There is a dustman who shapes our end, as Sir Winnie Churchill said, and it turned out to be a receipt from Pizer's warehouse."

"And what may that be?"

"Among other things four tough boys with coshes and two Alsatians trained to take the knackers off you when ordered. Maxie security, lot of wire cages of various sizes, all with nice locks on the door. Your stuff is safe at Pizer's if the busies want to take a look: they have to get a High Court order and by the time they get it the contents ain't there. It costs plenty, but it's better than a bank vault because Pizer don't muck about and no thief wants to lose his ears, which would happen if he tried to smash Pizer's. He doesn't want to *know,* just gives you a receipt. You take this to him and you can look at the stuff or take it away. If you haven't a receipt you're chucked out on your ear-'ole if not worse."

"What does the receipt say?"

"Just wire cage number sixty-one and the date. When you take the stuff away Pizer destroys the receipt. It's in Bermondsey, down between two alley-ways."

"Come on over," said Piron.

"I'll have to have my little bit of lunch."

"We'll have some on the way!"

He retold the conversation to Bardel, who said: "I've heard of Pizer. He is straight enough, but as you say he does not believe in sticky-beaking into the client's biz. Some dealers keep their wares there, and probably some burglars. Pizer would not be in any funny business personally."

When Hogg arrived he was in a sullen mood. Piron diagnosed that last night's sexual prowlings had been unsuccessful—nothing sours Hogg more than maidenly resistance or over-indulgence in vodka which he favours. Bardel had phoned for a taxi and sat with Hogg in the back. Piron stopped at a fried-chicken house where the waitresses, by chance, design or plain Act of God, had monstrous busts. This and fried chicken with sweetcorn patties restored Hogg's greasy face to as much complacency as it was capable of. Over coffee he confided: "There are two Pizers. One always sleeps there with the four night men and the dogs on duty. They eat in the place. It's got everything, electronic circuits, strong lighting, the best sprinkler system, safer than the bank."

Piron studied the receipt. It was a snide lawyer's creation with five hundred words in fine print. Pizer denied responsibility in all its forms beyond reasonable precautions.

The Pizer on duty was short and florid and was eating a smoked-salmon sandwich. He was obviously a compulsive eater for his waste-paper basket, in the glass cubicle which surveyed the large warehouse, was filled with discarded food containers.

He was friendly. "My guts have gone," he said, catching Piron's eye. "Wind around the heart like a kite in bad weather, but the worse it gets the hungrier I become. Bicarbonate, I'm full of it.

I try whisky but it only makes me fart so my wife's mother don't invite us any more."

"Here's a receipt," said Piron, producing it. "It doesn't say who took it out. You made no note of it."

"It's like bearer bonds or pork-belly futures," said Pizer, eating a peppermint. "You got the receipt, you got the stuff. I should care."

"Who put it in?"

"You get a judge in chambers, friend."

"A man was murdered!"

Pizer belched and looked faintly alarmed. "I don't like violence. I run a clean business. The law doesn't say I have to pry. You want stuff safely stored and I do it. Sure, I employ tough boys with dogs, but that is legal if they don't use more violence than necessary if somebody tries to break in. The man who brought the containers in was a guy who looked like a fish. One of the yobs, I thought, but so what?"

"Anybody look at it?"

"A man came in with the receipt six weeks ago. A Jew: a dealer I would say. He spent four hours in the cage. Here," he pressed one of the buttons on his desk top. With surprising alacrity a smartly dressed but very tough-looking man appeared.

"Nothing doing today, guv," he said.

"A gander looked at cage sixty-one six weeks ago," said Pizer.

The man's eyes slid over Piron, Hogg and Bardel. "A bit over four hours. There are cardboard cartons. He looked in each, gave me a fiddly as he went. He got away with nothing because I'm outside the wire watchin' the whole time. He weren't big when he came out, nothin' concealed under his coat or in his pants, trust me for that, guv'nor. I can see through ladies' skirts." He guffawed, and Piron just waited and stared. "He give me a pound for me trouble, said the man, "and I returned his receipt."

Piron produced a pound note, dangling it.

"He looked pleased, but in a narsty ol' way," said the man. "Like a busy man does when he 'as arrested his sister for being on the batter. I mighta thought 'e were a demon but for the fack that 'e was a little ol' yid. Right pleased about somethink he were." He took the pound.

"We'd better take a look," said Piron.

"I'll come personally," said Pizer. "Sometimes the exercise brings the wind up."

"Have you ever tried light ale?" asked Hogg.

"Never thought of it. Does it work?"

"My dad uses it. You can hear the result six streets away: the landlord says it's undermining the foundations and Dad has lost seven sets of teeth in four years and gets snaky letters from the National Health."

Pizer immediately dispatched one of his servitors to scurry out and procure a dozen bottles. Hogg stood beside him while Bardel worked away inside the seven square feet of heavy-duty wire. Piron, taking down the fifty cartons, noted that Pizer's eyes never left him for one second. There were three hundred and fifty pieces of silver in the boxes, ranging from a large pot with a crest on it, down to what might have been a snuff box with a rather explicit nude let into the inside of the lid.

"Rather a giveaway, that," muttered Bardel, "the snuff box is eighteenth century, or appears so, but that nude is the kind they were peddling in the eighteen thirties. Look at the legs! Still you never know, there were crowds of painters doing porno around seventeen fifty: one might have had an advanced technique. There is an old man at the Museum who knows every crack and crevice in such things and he'd know."

"What's the verdict?" asked Piron at last.

"Not proven by me," said Bardel. "Apart from the snuff box which I do not like. It could be genuine and if so the lot might fetch half a million."

Mr Pizer, who had not averted his eyes but quaffed a pint glass of light ale, emitted a gigantic postern blast. "You know, gents, it is bringing the wind up nice and steady, not in sudden bursts like, so as a bonus I'll tell you that the transaction stinks to me. Let's face it, men, the Warehouse and Depository is a bit of a drain, but I don't have to sniff around with me old snout, but occasionally you get a whiff, like a tube train in the rush hour. That's the bonus. Now, if you come out I'll give you back the receipt and reset the lock."

Frippingham was somnolent in the late afternoon sun. The concrete of the shopping centre was warm enough to penetrate the soles of Piron's moccasins as he walked with Hogg and Bardel towards the late McGregor's shop. It was open and Mr Snegg was polishing a grandfather clock with a felt cloth.

"Ah, good afternoon Mr Piron, and Mr Bardel is it not?"

"My assistant, Mr Hogg.'"

Snegg gave Hogg a slight nod and a clinical, schoolmasterish look.

"Business good?" asked Piron, more or less to cover up an awkward moment.

"For the time of year, not a good one, it is fairly steady. I had seven customers today and one particularly good sale, a matter of a pewter porringer which Mr McGregor had had for some years. Fashions come and go: today it's porringers and I wish we had more."

"We?" asked Piron.

"I have bought the business," smiled Snegg. "On terms over two years. It will be a stern struggle, but the Executors thought that on the whole they might accept my offer."

"I wish you well," said Piron. "I suppose you are renting the shop?"

"To buy the building would be absolutely beyond me."

"What we are here for is to enquire into the supposition that somebody entered the building by the main entrance to the apartments, went up the main stair, and down the back into McGregor's office."

"Do you mean Joyningstowe?"

"McGregor might or might not have been on to the Captain, but I doubt whether he would have informed. He did not dislike the man. And of course Joyningstowe had not bothered to junk his tools of trade which he surely would have if McGregor was a threat to him."

Snegg looked troubled. "I don't think," he said doubtfully, "that this sort of thing does a business any good, a point I made to the Executors when we discussed price. I had hoped it was over and, without being facetious, buried." He looked up as the door bell tinkled and Miss Traylor lurched in.

"Why, Mr Um, my gas stove still doesh not work, though there was another man at it yesterday," she greeted Piron, but fairly affably, as she swayed so that her battered shopping bag clanked.

"And what can I do for you, Miss Traylor?" asked Snegg.

"I've losht my key. Little small things today, not like we had at the school, great big things to keep the girls inside, their morals not being what they should be, in shpite, good gracious, of unremitting vigilance." By a drunken quirk Miss Traylor snapped to attention like a drill sergeant and her voice became crisp. "So having lost the street-door key, I shall have to go up the back stairs."

"Your apartment key," said Snegg. "Shall I get the locksmith *again*?"

"Now I keep it under the rubber doormat," said Miss Traylor, with dignity, "a simple thing that came to me in a dream. Mr McGregor will not mind."

"Mr McGregor had his throat cut," said Piron curtly.

"How curious," Miss Traylor slumped again, her eyes filming over. Then she brightened a little and pointed to Bardel. "This is the gentleman who did it, if I remember."

"I'll escort you upstairs," said Snegg, taking her elbow. "Perhaps you gentlemen will stay in the shop." He led her away.

"Funny how he wanted to get her away," said Hogg. "And what the hell is he buying a shop for at his age. He'll be moulderin' in 'is grave while the debt collector is knocking at the door."

"He might not be more than the fifties," said Piron. "He probably had to retire . . . over the ladies. Education departments do not mind it in reason but there are limits."

"Teachin' the young connubial joys, eh?" leered Hogg.

"I heard nothing like that," said Piron, but there were quick footfalls and Snegg came hurrying back.

"She is quite a problem," said Snegg, "always losing keys and hammering on my door late at night."

"The insurance company would hardly be amused."

"McGregor was not a fool. The small valuable stuff is kept in the vault, a modern one calculated to defy a professional for a couple of hours, and you can hardly make away with furniture. At night there is a microphone in the shop connected with a loud-speaker in McGregor's apartment, the kind of thing some people install in a nursery. Once," Snegg gave his dry chuckle, "Miss Traylor came down at four in the morning to let her old cat out, God knows why she chose to come this way. The cat, a nervous animal, mewed piteously and McGregor, convinced maniacs had broken in, telephoned the police who found old Traylor trying to open the shop door. The police were not amused."

"I do not think the local authority of Frippingham is noted for its sense of humour."

"Indeed not," said Snegg, "I worked for them for some years." His keen little eyes studied Piron.

"Jay Gould was sleeping with June Smith at the time McGregor was murdered."

Snegg licked his bottom lip. "I tried to give her advice," he said, "but the young ones will not listen to the voice of maturity today."

"You'd better go back," said Piron to Bardel and Hogg. "I have things to do."

At the White Horse his old friend gave him a warm greeting and a room for the night.

"A double, please," said Piron.

The landlord leered. "I shall have to inspect the Lines."

"They are tacked up in the bathroom of the flat."

The red-headed man put through a call. June Smith was

preparing to leave for her work. "We're staying the night at Frippingham, at the pub. Stick your spare knickers and my clean shirt in the overnight bag you'll find in the closet. What time does your stint end?"

"It's administrative stuff tonight. I could get forty minutes off for a quick meal."

"Tea for two, Alan, when the lady arrives."

"Do I know her?"

"One June Smith who teaches at the Tech."

"The mating of two redheads outvies as a spectacle the coupling of the Ceylonese elephants," said Alan solemnly, "upon the contemplation of which I shall buy you a drink. But why here? I mean, one thought poor old Joyningstowe had been unmasked and all that."

They went into the 'Snuggery', a part of the pub seemingly inhabited by embalmed old parties, seated in small club chairs and staring vacantly at double whiskies. You could have safely and openly plotted to blow up the whole Olympic Games in such a place.

"I'm not altogether satisfied about Joyningstowe," said Piron. "He forged quid notes for years at the rate of six per day, but does not seem to have had murderous instincts. Tell me, Alan, do you know a six-footer with a most charming smile, probably fiftyish, grey at the temples, curly brown hair, blue eyes, named Jack Prat, pronounced *Prah*?"

Alan sipped his vermouth and soda. "You see hundreds of people, mostly faceless, if you know what I mean. Their conversation is predictable and they come in mostly out of boredom. Still, it's my bread and butter. There was a man who met your description. It might have been three months ago. Drank Scotch and plain water, did not speak much, but I thought that he might be a Canadian, perhaps in real estate and taking a look at this locality. With him was a fish-faced Cockney, who I could not place. The kind you see near the door of a whore house. And who should come in and join them, but the pride of Frippingham, Master Jay Gould!"

"Did they talk?"

"Fish-face and the handsome Smiler exchanged a few thoughts about the weather. Just as Gould joined them I was called out to the kitchen to some disaster—I remember, the chef was drunk again. You have to tie him on a chair so he won't collapse and he gives instructions to the two assistants. I never saw the handsome man again, but—have another, you might need it . . ."

"You always were a ham, Alan."

"Actor manqué! Dad would not allow the thespian to come out in me. You know I try not to let out rooms, more trouble than it's worth with the staff position what it is. But this afternoon the fish-faced gentleman, giving the name of Brown, demanded accommodation. Some kind of sob stuff about his son being in Frippingham Hospital. He was the kind of type that can make trouble. I let him a room, next to the one in which you will wreak your wicked will."

"The lady is willing," murmured Piron, "at least on known form."

"Just to be annoying, not liking fish-faced men who are nasty in their manner, I phoned a pal at the hospital. There is only one Brown, a fifty-year-old whisky traveller with the D.T.s, hardly the scion of fish-face. I thought I would mention the matter to Mr Brown in the morning and suggest that he might care to move on."

"He is 'known' to the police," said Piron. "He could scarcely make trouble."

"I don't like the thought of him even staying overnight. Violent, is he?"

"When goaded into it. He is not the cold professional killer, though they are hard to come by and the ones you can get use so much cocaine they tend to mess it up."

They drank companionably until the barmaid answered the house phone. June Smith had arrived, and not in terribly good temper. Piron thought she had an ingrowing shrewishness, regrettable as it was becoming destructive to the natural beauty of her mouth. In a room off the kitchen, the landlord supervised the serving of steaks. After putting the sauce upon a hot plate he discreetly left the room.

"Beautiful steak," sighed June, "should not be consumed in forty minutes which is all I have."

"What have you been doing?"

"The smalls, talking with Mother on the phone." Practice made Piron think she was being less than honest.

"I discovered Mr McGregor's cache of silver."

"In the shop? He kept it in the vault."

"Not that lot. This was in a warehouse. His ex-wife had the receipt and sent it to me."

"I didn't know he had been married."

"She likes to dance and club."

June grinned. "Poor Julius! He was not a clubbable man, and the only dancing he enjoyed was engraved around pots, preferably Roman-Greek."

She finished her coffee after an interval of silence. "Was this silver valuable?"

"It depends. A lot of people buy these objects because they do not trust the monetary theories of our rulers who are employed at public expense to debase the currency. It is difficult to hedge. Land is best, but the prying hands of the State and inroads of deprived peasantry make that not quite safe. Beauty, however," and Piron leered, "is always saleable. I would rather have a Cellini salt cellar than the block of bricks which comprises our happy home. Only trouble with silver is that it is a little cumbersome if one has to flee abruptly."

"Where is it now?"

"In Pizer's warehouse, he being a philosopher who suffers from wind. You merely produce a receipt and take away the goods. Dead bodies are out, because Pizer goes around sniffing."

"How horrible!"

"You wait until Daddy leaves you his masterpieces. You'll be glad to store them with Pizer."

"Daddy has his money in armaments. Leonardos fade but a reliable Sten gun goes on for ever, and Daddy, in his inimitable way, says 'The nignogs will go on killing each other for three hundred years'. He is probably right: he generally is about money."

Piron looked at his watch. "I'll see you to the dark artistic mill."

"Don't bother. It is exactly twelve minutes and the males of Frippingham are too debilitated to contemplate rape."

A beautiful woman, all lusciousness, thought Piron fleshly as he saw her to the front door, but this did not prevent him seeing the landlord and being directed to the back delivery entrance. Frippingham centre was well lit, but Piron is adept at skulking, in practice a kind of listless walk which takes him into any available patch of shadow. June was maybe four minutes ahead, but it did not really matter, for Piron, jinking left, walked towards Jay Gould's studio. Opposite was a small self-service grocery store with a deep entrance between its windows. Into this he slipped.

Ten minutes later the girl emerged. Gould came down the steps with her and kissed her goodbye. Piron went back to the pub, consumed two brandies, and read a book upon his bed. He had taken care to slop brandy upon his chin, and when June returned about eleven he performed his drunken act, originally taught him by a very old timer who used to police American prohibition.

"I'm going along to the shop first thing tomorrow, say at nine. It might be as well, all things considered, to use your old flat," he said.

"The rent is paid for two months. Might as well." June put on her slippers.

"There could be important clues."

June did not comment but went out to the bathroom.

There was a pay telephone on the landing, Piron remembered. He waited until she returned, and in dressing-gown and a trifle staggery, he took his turn. The ear microphone of the handset was warm and there was a strand of auburn hair on it. He dialled Hogg's home, to be met by the assumed voice which Hogg put on until reassured that it was not an irate father or cuckolded husband.

"I have drifted a little bait, Hogg."

"My dad knew a third mate who liked to catch gummy shark. One day, instead of the bait, they took his you-know-what."

"You will be in McGregor's shop at nine tomorrow."

"Is there any danger, guv? I mean I'm not paid danger rate and if the cove what done old McGregor is present he might cut loose. It's all right for you senior citizens, but I've gotta couple of teenagers I'm chatting up and I don't want my looks altered."

"Nobody in their mortal senses would look at your face! Just be there at nine. I'll try to see that one of the doors is ajar."

"What do you expect?"

"That somebody will try to beg or buy or plain steal the receipt for the silver."

"That might mean bad trouble."

"Now Hogg, a black-listing from the Agency would mean you went clerking at half the money, you lacking many attributes for your vocation, which is poncing."

"You're a 'ard man, guv'nor. Very 'ard." When caught upon a dilemma Hogg's aspirates always went.

"Punctually at nine," said Piron firmly, and went back to bed.

"I suppose I had better go with you," said June over the breakfast table.

"As you like," replied Piron. "I dare say that not much will come out of it, but I have niggling doubts about the whole business."

They went in by the door to the apartments.

June's flat had a deserted look and already had the faintly musty smell of closed rooms. She opened the living-room windows. Looking out Piron saw Hogg standing below, massaging his acne and looking like a man on the point of departure.

"This is God!" roared Piron.

This proclamation had the usual fearful effect that it has on the English: Hogg goggled upwards and would doubtless have crossed himself except for his Free Church predilections.

"Come up, you bastard, to the third floor!"

"Who's that?" demanded June.

"London's most assiduous stud, my ugly assistant, Hogg." Piron went out into the corridor and felt oddly uneasy, but assumed a smile as Hogg sloped into view.

"The shop's shut, guv."

"What are you trying to do, lose your false teeth? McGregor used to open early because he was eccentric. People do not buy antiques before ten o'clock unless they are drunk. Snegg likes a peaceful life."

June Smith looked at Hogg with some curiosity. From a cheap three-day trip to Barcelona, Hogg had learned to kiss ladies' hands in a house of assignation, so he slobbered over one of hers. Piron thought that June looked harassed.

His attention thus diverted, he did not hear the door open and Mr Snegg walk in. He had probably learned the trick from spying on the schoolboys, thought Piron automatically as his eyes focused on the old fashioned 45-cal pistol which the elderly schoolmaster held quite expertly. Snegg gave his terrier grin. "I am quite at home with weapons," he said coolly, "having instructed during the war. Be quite still, will you." Perching himself on the side of an armchair, Snegg took professional precaution to be six feet away from Piron and Hogg. June Smith walked to the window, well out of the line of fire.

"I just want the receipt for that silver, Mr Piron."

"I have not got it."

"Dealing with generations of liars informs me that you have."

"Or dealing with informers."

"You might as well know that June is my wife—a marriage of convenience."

Piron said something unprintable, which aroused the pedagogue in Snegg. "There is a Trust," he said, "which falls to June if she marries before the age of twenty-six: that is next year. She wished to marry a sage but altruistic old party."

"Piron," said June, "it does something to you to see all that cake and just get a small slice. My father has cut me off without a penny: my mother is obtuse enough to remarry when he gets the final coronary—any man with a good line in chocolate liqueurs could accomplish hymeneal rights! But by marrying I get seventy thousand pounds, plus some property. I want to establish an art centre in Spain, do something worthwhile."

"For my part," said Snegg, "you can have no conception of a schoolteacher's frustrations. Brats into whose heads I pounded rudimentary knowledge ended up earning as much as five times more, let alone the politicians. This silver is worth a quarter of a million pounds and warmth and security for me."

"I suppose you murdered McGregor!"

"My dear sir, I thought that business was settled. Now, the receipt, please."

"You will have to take it."

"Mr Piron, in my profession we can rarely instil logic into our pupils. It would be easy for me to kill both you and the unpleasant pimply man with you. A shop with valuable stock, two men of—I fancy—dubious repute, witnesses to testify to threats."

"The gun might be difficult to explain."

"Not really. I found it in an old chest containing books. McGregor bought the contents of an attic and didn't get round to sorting them out. No, it is around sixty years old and hardly traceable, of Italian make and most probably a First World War souvenir. The point is that if I have to kill you, I shall simply say that one of you dropped it in a struggle and that I fired in self-defence. I shall have witnesses."

"June!" expostulated Piron.

"I really have no choice, Piron."

The door opened again. Piron was reminded of a famous American thriller writer who believed in having unpleasant people coming through doors at regular intervals and that nature usually follows art. It was Jay Gould looking resentful. He sidled along the wall to where June stood without turning her eyes from the street.

"My second witness," said Snegg and smiled. "Jay, who was Harry when I had the dubious pleasure of imparting knowledge to him, is a naughty boy who fulfilled his early promise. He has no choice but to do as I say. Forty years 'under the lock' as I believe they say, is the alternative."

"For Christ's sake get it over," mumbled Gould.

"I must relish my moment," said Snegg.

"You had better relish it quick," said June. "A big man with a crutch has entered the street door."

"Did you leave it open, Jay?" asked Snegg in the deadly silence.

"I thought we might want to get away quickly."

"You can rarely get away quickly," said Snegg, "except by killing yourself like Joyningstowe. A cunning man was he but it did not avail him. No, my dear Jay, we stay here."

There was the clumping of a crutch and a knock at the door. Snegg moved swiftly off the chair and carefully backed against the far wall, gun concealed behind his back.

"Come in!" ventured Piron.

It was Timothy Bardel, crutched stick under his left arm, protruding from a kind of cloak over his shoulders.

"Can I come in?" he said unnecessarily.

June turned towards him. "This is a convention called by my husband, Mr Snegg."

"Nothing like the joys of bountiful marriage," said Bardel, leaning against the closed door.

"Snegg has a gun," said Piron.

"I smelled something," said Bardel, "and I have a gun." He let the cloak drift from his right arm. There was a gun in his hand. Piron moved backwards leaving an angle between him and Snegg. Hogg foolishly blundered to the window, but Snegg seemed unperturbed.

"A late eighteenth-century duelling pistol," he said.

"My son likes working with his hands," said Bardel. "He took it to pieces and reassembled it. An antiquarian advised me on the gunpowder and ball. We've tried it in the back garden. Inaccurate, of course, though I have it aimed at your stomach. I need hardly tell you that the ball is soft lead and spreads rather horribly. Very few eighteenth-century people survived after a duelling wound."

Piron deliberately sniggered and Snegg's mouth turned white: the schoolmaster controlled his temper, but was obviously at a loss.

"We might as well settle this," said Piron. "Put your pistol very carefully on the shelf above you and we will talk in a relatively civilised manner."

Snegg looked his age, reached up behind his back, and put the gun on the ledge.

"You'd better give him a pat, Hogg," said Piron. "You see, Mr Snegg, carrying one gun and concealing another is an old trick."

Hogg, who does not like firearms, sneaked forward and patted. "He's clean, unless it's dangling where it couldn't be quickly reached."

"Well, gentlemen," said Snegg, again in command of himself, "what of it? You come here with a receipt owned by the late Mr McGregor, which is now my property."

"Forged silver!"

"I do not admit it but there is no offence in possessing reproduction silver."

"I don't know about that," said Piron, out of his depth.

"A court order might settle it!" Snegg was feeling confident. "But suppose we talk money. Ten thousand, contingent on sale, might interest you."

"We are getting out of here, Hogg." Piron's assistant made for the door whilst Piron backed to it slowly.

"Blimey, guv," said Hogg as they got outside, "Wot a dirty old swine, I swear he'd 'ave yer guts for garters."

Bardel, who had clumped slowly behind them said: "A large sum of money will corrupt any man."

"The bint made a rare fool of you, guv," sneered Hogg.

"I know it, little chap, but it was in some ways fun."

"Would he have shot?" asked Bardel.

"I think so," said Piron, "seeing that June Smith could not be forced to give evidence against her husband and Gould has something so nasty in his woodshed that he is Snegg's creature in every way."

"He wanted that receipt very badly," said Hogg, now recovered in aspiration. "I suppose it don't belong to anybody and finders are keepers." His nasty, close-set eyes sought Piron's.

"Trouble is that we are finders—adultery mostly—but not keepers."

"Keeping a respectable marriage bed costs a man enough," mourned Bardel. "There should be some reward accruing somewhere!"

"I don't know where the stuff came from," said Piron. "Jack Prat told me that McGregor was the seller, though I am inclined to wonder."

"Perhaps Prat had a client," said Hogg, "but he would find it difficult to explain how he got it. The answer to that one is to find a reputable dealer to act as the front. Prat might have bribed or conned McGregor into the position."

"Carrying on the thought," said Bardel, "we might suppose that McGregor entered into it in good faith, then smelled a rat."

They turned into the Police Station and waited twenty minutes for Inspector Feld, who was finishing up a report on the beating of a Hindu from Uganda by the League of British Patriots. "He's lost one eye," he told them, "and why can't the bastards stay away from Frippingham? You'd think they wanted a kick in the face. Bloody masochists!"

"In Australia they don't like policemen, in the States they don't like blacks, and my best friend is a Jew," soothed Piron.

Feld grinned, but sourly. "A policeman's lot . . . etcetera . . . Shakespeare was right."

"It was Gilbert, son of a necrophile, as all good policemen are because they know where the body is buried."

"You make me laugh, Piron," said Feld, quite genuinely, "Piron's purple pills make life seem fun. But I have the gloomy thought that your theories are going to glow like grog blossoms."

"Only that I think that Snegg probably killed McGregor."

"The case is closed, Piron. I do not wish to hear more about it."

"This is on record?"

"The report is filed. And it has been so nice to meet you that I pray I shall never have to again."

"It might be profitable to keep a tag upon Snegg," persisted Piron. "A nice, well-established antique shop would offer the ideal outlet for certain stolen goods."

"Profitable for whom?" asked Feld, with a flash of irritation. "I run this station on a bloody budget and an acreage of 'please explain' memos. There is no organised crime in Frippingham, even the whores are in private practice, a fact which my accountant masters relish to tickle me with if I sanction overtime. I cannot put Snegg under any detailed surveillance as far as his shop-keeping activities are concerned."

Piron shrugged and they left. Bardel and Hogg, the latter keeping close to the man with the gun, went to fetch Bardel's old car. At the White Horse Piron packed his bag and went to pay his bill. "The lady will be collecting her own traps," he told the publican.

"A rift in the lute?"

"With two o's."

"Funny undertones around here, occasionally, though there always are in a pub."

Alan made change. "The fish-faced man that I was aiming to politely eject went early this morning, without breakfast, though he paid for it."

Piron thanked him and went out to the car. Bardel, by his own little van, limped over. "I owe the Agency money, Piron. Would you set a few days' work against it? I'm mobile and," he chuckled, "can travel with duelling pistol."

"I 'ope it's registered," said Hogg, cravenly, "the beaks giving fourteen years to them what haven't the sussificate."

"We are going to lend two, at a profit, to the C.I.A.," said Piron. "Go with Bardel and I'll join you at Pizer's."

It was a beastly drive and two o'clock showed on Piron's watch as he parked outside the warehouse. A different member of the Pizer clan greeted him and glanced at his card. Hogg and Bardel were already inside the glass cubicle.

"I know Mr Bardel," said this Pizer, a bald, thin strip of a man, "on account of him doing business for me once in the enquiry way. We don't want to know anything about this particular cage, but if you have the receipt you can take the stuff away. There is a matter of sixty-nine pounds owing."

"How are you paid?" asked Piron.

Pizer looked at him like a death's head. "We ask for a deposit in cash, thereafter a three-monthly settlement in cash. Sometimes they come in, more often it is a messenger. We give a written receipt made out to the cage number. No names are ever involved, we take care to avoid that."

"I heard that often, if the police come round, the appropriate cage is empty, the booty flown to another nest."

Pizer shrugged. "Some, not all, of the people who use us have noses like hawks, to continue your simile. If police are prowling, the receipt is presented and the contents of the cage taken away."

"Suppose it is taken by someone who is not the rightful owner?"

"Read the fine print, Mr Piron. We paid a hundred quid to Sir Eric Sloughbody Q.C. to vet it when we were starting. No liability at all on our part."

"I'll give you the receipt and take the stuff away."

"You are a bit of a special case, Mr Piron," said Pizer, lighting a Dutch cigar, "because I cannot say, as I usually do, that I do not know you. You'd better give me a little memo in writing to the effect that you are the legitimate custodian of the contents of cage sixty-one. You can put it on this letterhead."

Piron scribbled legal terms..

"Very nice, Mr Piron," said Pizer, "very succinct, to coin a phrase. As a bonus I'll tell you that an hour ago a nasty young man came in and demanded the contents of the cage. He said the receipt had been lost. When I laughed he turned abusive, so," he pressed the little button on the desk and a huge, raw-boned man came trotting across the warehouse floor. Piron recognised him as Big Bertie Strout, a brainless animal of the slums whose muscles had made him a living since he was dismissed from an Army Glasshouse.

"The fish-faced man, you put him out?" asked Pizer.

"He had a razor," said Strout, "so I had to take him by the short hairs. He saw the light pretty quick, as our dear old chaplain at Aldershot used to say. He had a van and drove away in it. I seen 'im before some place, all wind and water and tits and temper as they are today. Grip 'em where it hurts and you hear a dufferent tale, I say a dufferent tale. Grip 'em . . ."

"Thank you Bertie," interposed Pizer. "There'll be a little bit of nice in your pay packet come Thursday." The big man shambled out.

"They beat him on the head with rubber truncheons," said Pizer, "until his brains jellied. He's an animal, but in the lion class. If I told him to go into a burning building, he'd go. Lot of men about like that! Trouble is their brains have gone and they are like discs playing over and over again. But he wouldn't allow you near a cage except on me or my brother's say-so. You should have seen the way that fish-faced feller looked at him, evil like, but then one of the guard dogs came into sight and he packed it up."

"He might help us load the boxes," said Piron, "and I'd like another boy and a dog to guard the van we've got while we are stowing it away. And now for your bill." He produced his cheque book.

It took half an hour to stack the boxes in the van. Hogg timorously ventured that he 'didn't want to 'ave a bar of them bleedin' boxes' and so took the car back to the office. Piron went in the passenger seat of Bardel's van and they drove to Scotland Yard. It was a tiresome, cluttered progression. Eventually Bardel waited behind the wheel, while Piron, encountering red-tape difficulties owing to the presence of a van not supported by public funds, eventually got in to see the old Superintendent.

His friend was somewhat less than pleased when Piron requested him to have the silver stored.

"Damn it, we're not a depository."

"Suppose . . ." started Piron.

"Nor a goddamn suppository either." The Super was mad, his pipe wobbling from the corner of his mouth.

"Suppose it is stolen property."

"And since when did you receive stolen property?"

"I received, quite legitimately, a receipt upon Pizer's Warehouse. Pizer told me that a sinister character, probably the Dickybird, had demanded the contents of the wire cage. So I brought the stuff here. If genuine it might be worth anything from two hundred thousand of Barber's baubles upwards."

"Who gave you the receipt?"

"Do you really want to know? I should prefer not to tell you."

"Much as I love you, Piron, you won't get out of here without making a statement, preferably before a Justice of the Peace. My pension is coming up in three months . . ."

"It was Mrs McGregor, relict of the late Julius. He gave it to her for safe keeping. Love had gone through the window, but some business remained."

"You suppose he was killed for it, I presume?"

"McGregor was notorious for carrying his private papers in a bulging wallet. The murderer was in no position to know that McGregor had a back-stop in his ex-wife. A dealer, a refugee from tyranny, develops habits such as carrying in person as much of his business as possible. When the local Inspector showed me the report, it mentioned that the wallet was in a drawer in the desk. They did not attach any importance to it, as there was six hundred pounds in it, which tied up with what his written accounts seem to point to."

"We'll have to get a J.P.," said the Super.

The J.P., a smallish man with a ginger moustache, arrived. Piron dictated a preliminary statement and, with Bardel as supervisor and two constables as carriers, transferred the boxes into a dismal little, cell-like room and signed various additional papers.

When they drove away, Bardel was in good form in spite of the odour of stale embrocation which Piron found trying as his friend exercised an Englishman's prerogative to keep windows firmly shut, the windows in the driving compartment being hermetically sealed by adhesive tape. Additionally, gloomed Piron, one bathroom and eight children plus a wife did not give Bardel opportunity enough to wash as often as he might like.

"Can we park near the Madeleine Hotel?" he asked.

"There's a delivery area. I know old Percy, the yardman. It might cost a pound, but none of the higher flunkeys'll take much notice of a beat-up old van like this. What is it all about?"

"There is a Gerald Savory, an American who lives by his wits, strictly non-violent, and his girl friend Valerie, who you might say charitably has lived by *her* wits. They are fronts for selling the silver and they seem to be the joker in the pack, the point being that they state they are employed by Jack Prat whereas McGregor had the receipt. I want a witness, so you might come up with me."

"For another quid we could use the service lift—it runs to the storeroom on each floor."

The yardman, as yardmen are, was of morose temperament, put upon, incompetent and open to bribery. But two quid and Bardel's professional whining about his stick got them into the clanging service lift, a relic of hydraulic craft. Gerald Savory answered Piron's rap on the door of the suite. Inside was the atmosphere of departure.

"We're almost on our way." Savory was surly. There were open suitcases on the floor. Valerie smiled up at them from the floor.

"This is Tim Bardel," said Piron. "He was in McGregor's shop shortly after his throat was cut."

"I thought he carried his head funnily," cooed Valerie as she gave a professional smirk, bending so that her good legs were very visible.

"The throat in question was the late McGregor's, darl, who apparently owned or had custody of the silver. And quit the light-hearted talk and pull your frock down."

"It's nothing to me, having eight to provide for," said Bardel, a trifle wistfully, so Piron thought.

"We told you," said Savory. "It belongs to Mr Jack Prat."

"I give you notice that I cleared the wire vault at Pizer's out a couple of hours ago."

Savory's little bug-eyes momentarily flashed, like a cat's when a car passes. "Nothing to us," he said, quickly.

"If the rightful owner were found there might be a reward."

"Is not 'going to your reward' one of your nice limey ways of saying somebody's had their throat cut?" asked Valerie, as she folded a drip-dry shirt.

"Jack Prat would know," warily said Savory, like a trout at a fly, "he is the middleman. I had no knowledge that it might be hot."

"It has some value," said Piron. "My friend Bardel knows a lot about old silver, and he thinks at least some of it was genuine, and probably the rest is first-class repro."

"We'll let it be. The sooner I'm back home in the cosy whorehouse with my shoes off the better." Valerie did not look up from her packing.

"Maybe that is best," said Piron. "So long."

"You are leading with the chin, Piron," said Bardel as they went down to the parking area. "The little rat will be on the blower to Jack Prat, who is not the man to tamper with."

"I've already tampered," replied Piron. "We had better stop at my apartment. Take the van round the back and come up for a drink."

While Piron poured two beers Bardel lurked with professional expertise at the side of the curtains. "The Dickybird," said Bardel, "in the bookshop opposite, strategically placed so that he can peer through the window."

"He must have come partly by subway," said Piron, "thus beating the traffic. I suppose we have an hour."

"What shall we do?" asked Bardel and Piron chuckled before he spoke.

It was forty-five minutes before the front-door bell rang. Piron winked at Bardel before he went to answer it. It opened inwards and he stood slightly to one side.

"Piron!" The voice was soft and transatlantic.

"Valerie!" Piron took the chance and moved back. "What are you doing, and if you have anybody with you just come in peaceable."

"I'm alone." She looked quite elegant as she stepped through the door.

"Bardel is with me, drinking beer."

"The gas will do you no good! Better get out of here while the going is good."

"What do you drink, Valerie?"

"Rum, but don't be a fool."

"We have a good Bacardi."

"Piron, Savory, like the craven-hearted punk he will always be, hit me under the jaw . . ." she pointed and Piron saw a patch of red underneath her ear. "He grabbed a valise, the money, made a hurried call to Jack Prat while I lay there pretending to be out to it, and made off. He always carries his passport on him. He'll be on the next available flight to New York. Prat's boys will be here any tick of the clock."

"Come into the living-room and partake. Your nerves are shot."

Bardel looked at Valerie without much favour as Piron mixed her a drink.

"Valerie told me," said Piron, "that Savory knocked her down, phoned Jack Prat and made off."

"They want that silver," said Valerie, "and, Buster, Prat will put the first league in. He's got a hood named Darcy Angel."

Angel, ticked Piron's memory bank, a man of dubious nationality but with American papers that the Justice Department had not been able to disprove. He was currently in the smoke after the killing of a Mafia Chieftain. He spoke French, Spanish and Italian and was adept at disguise, easier now that wigs proliferated. A hardened professional killer, squat and muscular.

"Angel is wanted back home for questioning."

"Therefore," said Valerie, "he needs the money to keep away. You get these hit boys and they are desperate, so you have a cobra. Get out the back way, men, and take me."

"We'll enjoy our tot."

"What are you up to, Piron? Are the cops staked out?"

"Mr Prat has a watcher outside."

"I'd better get," Valerie set down the drink untouched, "not wishing to be in a plastic-surgery ward."

"Better to stay put than run away," said Piron. "At least it often works that way."

"Then, for God's sake, give them the silver, which is all they want."

"There is some money in it, dearie. There is a man named Snegg, who undoubtedly killed old McGregor. He cannot claim the silver unless he wishes to risk a possible charge of murder. Let us take a look at Jack Prat. Suppose he was the front for a massive confidence trick, based on a lot of unemployed silversmiths. Even assuming the growing weakness of Wilson's Wampum and Teddy's Treasure the operation could have been immensely profitable. As I see it, Prat lied when he said that McGregor was the vendor. Prat conned McGregor into being the intermediary, owing to his good reputation.

"A sprinkling of the stuff is genuine, but most of it is first-class reproduction, or so I think. There have been quite a lot of unemployed craftsmen, one of whom was murdered abroad—the connection is not proven. But there was a dubious middleman named Forrest who was shot dead when he tried to pry, I suppose by Darcy Angel. Snegg's greed was pivotal. He and his wife, with the aid of a punk named Jay Gould, steered McGregor into the transaction, possibly by the aid of a dishonest 'expert'. However, McGregor was a strange, devious man who liked what I can only describe as cynical parody. He knew what they were doing: and at the right moment he was going to blow the whole thing up, but Snegg got in first. Then it was Snegg negotiating with Jack Prat."

"An elegant exposition, Mr Piron." Jack Prat, groomed and smiling, had opened the door. Behind him came in a squat, swarthy man; Darcy Angel, registered Piron. There were two more, the fish-faced Dickybird, and a small, efficient-looking black man who seemed rather bored.

"We came in the back, Piron," said Prat. "I have a small listening device which I glued to the door, to hear your excellent summary."

"Do we have to do the stand-up bit!" Darcy Angel had a deadpan mid-western voice.

"My dear fellow, we must observe propriety."

"But not the law of property," grunted Piron.

"What a wag you are," said Prat admiringly. "Just hand over the silver! You'll all be administered a bit of a bashing thereafter, but it won't be too bad. It's just that nobody gets in Jack Prat's road without a share of punishment."

Valerie began to cry. Prat looked at her sadistically as she groped in her handbag.

Darcy Angel was first league, you had to hand him that. With economy of effort, he stepped forward as her hand darted out with a small pistol in it, and twisted her wrist so that the weapon bounced on the carpet. Piron remained still as the black man crowded him, hand in one pocket.

"We'll settle the score later," said Prat. "Now where is the silver, Piron? You are too old a hand not to know the uselessness of argy-bargying."

"In my bedroom," lied the red-headed man, looking sullen.

"You and I, Dickybird, will accompany Piron to inspect. You other two remain here. I do not, period do not, want any noise."

"There would not be any noise if the windpipes were cut," said Darcy Angel professionally.

"For God's sake," said Prat, "I do not want cut windpipes."

"I wish you'd make your mind up, Mr Prat. We can't afford to be amateurish."

"Wait until we come back," said Prat.

"Come along, Piron," said the Dickybird, drawing a switchknife, "and remember I love you like a brother."

Piron went first along the narrow hallway. He carefully pulled his key ring from his trouser pocket, unlocked the door and pushed it in. Four men, rather scholarly looking, in overalls came out. Three had rubber truncheons, the fourth a gun. Piron chopped Prat to his knees, while the Dickybird boggled.

"Shouldn't have used violence, Mr Piron," said the Detective Sergeant, as he dexterously put the cuffs on the Dickybird, accidentally treading on his feet in the process.

"You goddamn fool." Prat, harder physically than he looked, got on his feet and cursed the Dickybird, who whined something unintelligible.

"He's not to blame," said Piron. "These police officers came in a truck marked 'Town Council' with rubbish collection bins on the back. I am laying a charge against you for trespass with intent to commit a felony, and the same for one Darcy Angel and a black man in my living-room."

A resourceful professional, Angel made no attempt to run. As well as Valerie's pistol, a larger one was on the carpet.

"Police here," said the Sergeant.

"My friend and me was invited as guests, for a convivial drink," said Angel.

"And you carrying a convivial gun," said Piron, touching the thirty-two with the toe of his left shoe.

"Never seen it before," said Angel and his companion shook his head.

"Angel dropped it on the floor," said Bardel.

"Two words against two," leered the gunman.

"I'm charging you with trespass with felonious intent," snapped Piron.

"We deny trespass, but if we have committed any damage we will pay for repair," responded Prat smoothly. "Felony, is, of course, a myth invented by Piron."

"There will be two police cars by now," said the Sergeant. "We will all depart for Scotland Yard."

"We can make the trespass stick," said the old Superintendent as Piron, at midnight, was preparing to leave, "but the felonious intent is out. Your witnesses would hardly stand up. This Valerie woman is a whore from Las Vegas. Bardel is, from your word, honest enough, but a private detective—a term redolent of shady pastures."

"Thanks," said Piron.

"Not you, Piron," the Super scrambled back to the dry land. "An international corporation with links with both the C.I.A. and the F.B.I. is vastly different."

"Don't you forget the Daughters of the American Revolution, we guard the honour of their daughters."

"Which Revolution? The Permissive one?" The old Super was a well-known wag.

"But seriously, Piron, the value of that silver, according to the bloke we got in, is about seventeen thousand pounds, maybe five per cent more. If there is no claimant I guess it belongs to Mrs McGregor."

"Less ten per cent for the Agency, which will be split with Bardel," said Piron. "A dirty case, with all the rogues still at large."

"It's nearly always that way," said the Super. "Nearly always, but I do keep a bottle of Scotch in the Pending file."

So it was two hours later that Piron arrived home, having dropped off the Super en route. The flat had a used look. There was the faint smell of June's bath essence in the bedroom. He wandered around, drained, but the door bell rang. He had locked the back door and the front was now on the chain.

Cautiously Piron peeked through the viewing device.

"Oh, God!" he muttered and opened up.

Valerie looked remarkably pretty and carried an overnight bag. "I've nowhere to go, Piron," she replied.

"Come in, the central heating is turned up."

"The Wages of Death is Sin, Piron," said Valerie.